BURN

A WITCHBANE NOVELLA

MORGAN BRICE

CONTENTS

BURN

By Morgan Brice

ISBN: 978-1-939704-79-5

Cover art by Lou Harper.

Darkwind Press is an imprint of DreamSpinner Communications, LLC

1

EVAN

"What do you mean, you've got a surprise for me?" Evan Malone's tone was wary. "The last big surprise involved armed men shooting up my apartment before they burned it down."

His boyfriend, Seth Tanner, winced a bit at that, and Evan wished he could take back the words. "I didn't mean—"

Seth managed a smile. "It's okay. And…it's true. But this is a good surprise. Even if it's kind of connected to that other time."

Now Evan was really confused, but he let Seth lead him from the bedroom of the fifth-wheeler RV they shared out to the living room. With an electric fireplace, flat screen TV, and cushy leather furniture, it was easy to forget that their home was on wheels. On the table in the dining area was a large box and two smaller ones.

"It's not Christmas—or my birthday," Evan said, glancing at Seth again, who shooed him on with an expression Evan didn't quite understand, something between pleased and sad.

"Open them."

Evan saw that the boxes weren't taped shut, so he went

for the big one first, indulging his inner ten-year-old. The new laptop inside made him catch his breath. "Seth—"

"You still have two more."

Biting back a comment, Evan opened the next biggest box to find a good quality, SLR digital camera, definitely capable of taking professional photographs. Knowing Seth would object if he didn't finish his task, he opened the smallest box to find a cell phone.

"I wanted to replace what got destroyed in the fire," Seth said. "If I'd gotten to you sooner, maybe that wouldn't have happened," he added, self-recrimination thick in his voice. "Anyhow, now you can start up that graphic design business you talked about, and be able to do photography for it. And, you know, take calls." He looked nervous, and Evan realized he had been so thunderstruck he hadn't reacted.

"I didn't expect...wow. This is why you were asking so many questions about what kind of equipment I used to have?" he asked, and Seth nodded, still looking a little off. "Thank you. But...I can't let you pay for all this."

"It's my fault what you had got destroyed."

Evan met Seth's gaze. "If you hadn't gotten me out of there, I wouldn't have made it, either. Not your fault, Seth. You were the freakin' Terminator." He dropped his voice. "Come with me if you want to live." That managed to get a wan smile from Seth that did not reach his eyes.

When Evan thought about that night, he figured his description was only a slight exaggeration. He and Seth went back to his apartment after a date, had really good sex, and fell asleep together. When armed intruders had broken through the door shouting for "Jackson Malone"—his full name—Seth had fired back, blocked the goons, then got Evan out the window and whisked him away on his black Hayabusa cycle.

"Do you like them?" Seth asked, and Evan heard the doubt in his voice.

"I love them. You must have been taking notes. They're newer versions of what I had—and what I need," Evan said. He put down the phone and wrapped his arms around Seth, letting his head fall into the crook of Seth's neck. He was almost exactly the same height as Seth—just a bit shorter— something that had never been true of his other lovers. He found that he liked how perfectly their bodies aligned.

"You said that if you left Treddy's, you wanted to start your own business. So now you can. It'll be something you can do on the road. Or...wherever." Again, Evan heard the uncertainty in the other man's voice.

"Hey," he said quietly, stepping back just enough to be able to see Seth's face, still remaining in the circle of his arms. "I'm not planning to go anywhere without you. There's nothing in Richmond for me now." When Seth winced, Evan shook his head. "I couldn't go back to Treddy's, not after Jackie sold me out. And it'll be months before it reopens, anyhow." He sighed. "I think I've mentioned about a hundred times that I knew I needed to get on with my life. Tending bar was just a way-station until I found a new direction."

Seth smiled, and this time, the affection reached his eyes. He leaned forward and kissed Evan, a brush of lips across his, but enough to send heat straight to Evan's groin. "I just want to make sure that this," he said, gesturing to the RV as if implying everything that came with it, "is really what you want to do."

Evan knew how loaded the question was for Seth. Since Seth's brother Jesse was murdered two years ago, Seth had dedicated his life to tracking down the culprits—an unknown number of witch-disciples to a dark warlock dead for over a century, avenging their leader's death in a cycle of ritual murders targeting the descendants of the sheriff's deputies who killed him. Evan was the first of the descendants Seth tried to save, and in the process, they had fallen in love. At least, Evan hoped that what seemed so clear and true in the intensity of fighting for their lives would prove to be real for the long run.

"I want to have your back," Evan said, stretching up to kiss Seth's stubbled jaw. "I want to help you stop the other descendants from getting killed—put an end to this once and for all. I want to keep you safe so we can get to the 'happily ever after' part." He had punctuated each comment with a kiss, and claimed Seth's lips after the last one, adding a little more heat as he ran his tongue over the seam of Seth's mouth, begging for entrance.

Seth opened to him, and Evan licked into his mouth, in a kiss that was tender and claiming. Seth tasted of coffee and mint toothpaste, and he smelled like vanilla shampoo with a hint of lemon soap. Seth groaned and pulled Evan closer, slotting them together. Despite their wake-up sex not long ago, Evan could feel the press of Seth's erection against his hip, letting him know that he was ready for another round.

"I love you," Seth murmured, then licked the shell of Evan's ear, sending a shiver through him that had nothing to do with cold. "I just want you to be happy."

"And I choose to be here, with you, doing what we do, so I *am* happy," Evan replied, nuzzling against Seth's neck, inhaling his scent. He ran a hand up through Seth's short, blond hair, as Seth tangled his fingers in Evan's longer, dark strands. Evan's stomach rumbled, reminding him that there were primal needs other than sex. "But right now, I'm starving. So…food first?"

Seth chuckled and dropped a kiss on Evan's forehead before stepping back. "And a rain check on the other stuff," he promised.

The RV's galley kitchen had all the important equipment, packed into a compact space. That made it difficult for two men to move around at the same time. Seth was broad-shouldered with plenty of muscle honed by time in the military and a grueling fitness regimen he maintained to keep him in shape so he could fight the supernatural creatures they hunted. At six-three and two-twenty, Seth took up his share of space. But while Seth had thirty more pounds of muscle, Evan wasn't exactly small, even if he had a more slender build and a runner's physique. Tight quarters made for plenty of acci-dentally-on-purpose crotch-to-ass slides that added spice to the process of cooking a meal and set the stage for sweet after-dinner activities.

Dinner wasn't fancy—spaghetti with meat sauce, a bagged salad, and garlic bread from the freezer, but it filled the RV with luscious aromas and made Evan's stomach rumble even more. Evan looked around at the trailer. Seth's parents bought it for a retirement they didn't live to enjoy. Seth had added some touches of his own, but it still felt like he had borrowed it from someone else. Maybe in time, if this thing between them worked out, Evan could help him make it feel more like theirs.

Two weeks had passed since Seth defeated the witch-disciple in Richmond and saved Evan's life. They had gone north to Fredericksburg, to a proper campground with elec-tric and water hookups instead of squatting at an abandoned farm. The family-owned park wasn't fancy, but it had a fire pit and grills, as well as a rec room and a small convenience store, concession stand, and vending machines. The pool was closed for the season, but Evan could imagine kids playing and parents lounging on chairs nearby.

"Are you in there?" Seth snapped his fingers. Evan real-ized he'd been lost in thought.

"Yeah, just…wondering what the next stop is on the Magical Mystery tour," Evan said. They had been glad to get away from Richmond in the wake of what happened and drove north until they found an open park. Most of the time since then had been recovering and easing into a relationship, a mixture of sex, sleep, and tentative conversation.

They were still both dancing around each other. Now that Evan wasn't targeted for death by a psycho warlock, their initial reason to stay together was gone. In the intensity of their struggle to live through the fight with the killer, their emotions had been high, and they had declared their love for one another. It all *felt* genuine. Evan had never fallen so hard, or so fast before. He didn't think Seth had, either. But when the adrenaline finally subsided, would they still feel the same?

"Everything we've found makes me think the next witch-disciple is near Pittsburgh," Seth said, pushing his plate away and wiping his mouth with a napkin. He went to the fridge and came back with a beer for both of them. "Technically, we have until next Halloween. But—"

"But why not pick him off early and go on to the next one?" Evan supplied.

"That was my thought."

Seth's phone rang, and he answered. "Hi, Toby. What do you have for me?" Evan could hear the older man's voice, although the words were muffled. "We're near Fredericks-burg. Need us to do something?" He listened for a while, nodding. "We can definitely take care of that. And thanks for the intel. That helps."

He paused again. "Yeah, he's here. Breaking him in to life on the road." That look came back again, sad and something else, before vanishing. "Killjoy," he chuckled. "'Cause I'm sure you and Milo wouldn't if you had the chance. On second thought, I don't want to know! I'd need to bleach my brain. Some things can't be unseen." Toby said something else, and Seth nodded. "You too. Give my best to your better half." He ended the call and stayed silent for a while.

"Hello? What was that all about?" Evan asked after the minutes dragged by.

Seth shook off his wandering thoughts. "Toby says that there've been some reports of a vengeful haunting near here.

He was going to put it out to someone else, but it might be good for us to take it; you know, on the job training. Get your feet wet on something simple."

Evan restrained himself from reminding Seth that just a few weeks ago, his feet had been very wet—with blood. They'd cut it fine and nearly hadn't survived the encounter. But if Evan was serious about being in Seth's life, then stopping dangerous supernatural threats—aside from murderous witch-disciples—was part of the bargain. His heart thudded at the prospect, but if he couldn't handle hunting, he and Seth had no future.

"I'm game," he said, hoping his smile looked whole-hearted. "What was Toby razzing you about?"

Seth's cheeks pinked. "Ah...he wondered how we were getting on in our little mobile 'passion pit.'"

Evan sputtered on his beer. "He said that?"

Seth nodded, grinning. "Yeah, and he must have made a list of other phrases because I don't think he's clever enough to just whip off one after another. "Sex on wheels. Horny home away from home—"

"I get the picture," Evan said, laughing. Toby and Milo were probably older than Seth's parents, a husband-and-husband hunter team who had helped Seth in his early days when he had been blind with the need for vengeance but clueless about the things that went bump in the night. They had trained Seth, helped him find allies in the close-knit community he could trust, and treated him like an adopted son. Evan hadn't met them, but he knew how much they meant to Seth.

"Tell me about the ghost." Evan tried to sound business-like. He hoped he didn't look fidgety. He'd meant what he said about having Seth's back. If Seth didn't think Evan could handle himself, he wouldn't trust him as his partner—on the job, or in bed.

"This whole area is lousy with historic houses," Seth said,

pausing to take a swig of his beer. "Sometimes, the dearly departed residents don't want to move on. If they aren't causing problems, that's fine. But there's an old mansion that's been turned into a B&B. Apparently, it has a hell of a history...maybe for real. The ghost is strong enough to do real damage, and people are getting hurt."

He toyed with the half-empty bottle. "At first, it was workmen doing renovations. A guy almost got killed when something winged a hammer at his head in an empty room. Luckily, he ducked."

"He's sure no one else could have been there?"

"The guy was working on the lock on the inside of the door, which was shut with his body blocking it from opening, and he says he was alone. The hammer put a hole right through the door."

"Shit."

Seth nodded. "Yeah. There'd been reports from some of the real estate agents who showed the place about being pushed on the stairs, having things fall near them. A lot of the agents refused to show the place, even though it had a nice price tag. The new owners thought it was all just stories and people's imaginations until the husband got pushed out a second-floor window. There were witnesses. They said an invisible force threw him against the glass. He was my size."

"Sweet baby Jesus. Did he die?"

"No, but he got very lucky. The workmen walked off the job—understandable. The new owners are stuck with a hefty mortgage, and they obviously can't open to the public. The bank is afraid they'll default and leave them on the hook for the property—again," Seth added. "So apparently, someone in the bank went looking for a ghostbuster. Tried the local mediums and psychics—nothing wrong with that. For a low-level problem, it can work. But they weren't successful."

"Let me guess," Evan chimed in. "Someone in Toby and Milo's circles eventually heard about it—and here we are."

"Yeah. That's usually how it works. I've got a job to finish for a client, but it'll probably only take me the morning to wrap up," Seth replied. He'd been in computer ops in the Army and used those skills as a hunter to get into police databases and other locked down sites when need be. Toby had convinced Seth to establish himself as a "white hat" hacker, getting hired by companies to stress test their computer systems and keep out the riff-raff. It paid well and was a job he could do on the road, from anywhere.

If Evan could get his design and photography business off the ground, it would be a dream come true. He hadn't been using his degree or following his heart working at Treddy's bar. He'd found a shelter in the storm after he moved to the Richmond to escape a stalker, and never moved on. Now he had a real chance to do what he loved, with a man he loved. And in his spare time, risk his life to kill off supernatural predators most people didn't believe even existed.

Then again, every job has its trade-offs, he thought, trying to convince himself he was up for it.

"What's the plan? Just walking up and knocking on the door might not be a good idea," Evan said. He'd spent four terrifying days running for his life from a faceless threat, only to walk right into the warlock's trap and nearly become his latest sacrifice. Seth had tried back then to teach him the basics about supernatural self-defense, but Evan had to admit that his initial wariness and skepticism meant he hadn't paid attention as closely as he should have.

"Still working on that part," Seth admitted. "But I'll come up with a plan." His fingers brushed against Evan's hand on the table. "So..." he let his voice trail seductively. Seth slipped his sock-clad foot up Evan's inseam, gently kneading between his legs.

"I like how you think."

"Did you have something in mind?" Seth asked, teasing.

Evan rose to his feet and moved sinuously to stand

9

between Seth's spread legs. "I don't think I thanked you properly for your surprise," he said with a wicked grin. He sank to his knees and began to nuzzle the inside of Seth's thigh, letting his hot breath sink through the denim.

Seth groaned and slouched in his chair, letting his legs splay wider. Evan took his time, mouthing at the now-damp cloth, nipping lightly, in no hurry to reach his groin.

"You're welcome. Now get to the good stuff," Seth made a move to unbutton his fly, but Evan batted his hand away.

"Bossy bottom," Evan said with a chuckle. He didn't hurry, just continued his sweet torture until he reached Seth's now-prominent bulge. "Hmmm." He wrapped his lips around the outline of Seth's cock through the denim and hummed.

"God. You're killing me, here."

"That's the point."

"If I cream my jeans, just remember—it's your week to do laundry."

"That's a risk I'm willing to take." Evan flicked open the top button and swiped his tongue along the sliver of skin above the waistband as Seth arched back. This time, Seth didn't attempt language, just moaned to encourage Evan's progress. Another button, then a third, and Evan paused to mouth Seth's stiff prick through his boxer briefs.

Evan ran his tongue over the head, still covered by cotton cloth, and tasted where the pre-come had soaked through the fabric. Another button undone, then one more, and Seth lifted up so Evan could pull his jeans down to his ankles and kicked them free.

Evan went to work in earnest, pressing his nose and lips against Seth's sac, mouthing his balls and breathing in the musky scent that was soap and pre-come and uniquely Seth.

"Not gonna last. Please—"

Evan pulled down Seth's briefs, and his swollen cock bobbed free, dripping a sticky trail. Seth gasped as the cool air hit hot flesh, then cried out as Evan swallowed him down to the root in one move.

Seth's cock hit the back of Evan's throat, and then Evan slowly pulled back, letting his tongue swirl over the sensitive velvet skin, seeking out the tender spot beneath the head, and slipping through the slit. Seth tangled his fingers in Evan's hair, twining around the chestnut strands that were the perfect length to give him a good grip.

Evan deep throated him again, and this time, he slipped a hand between Seth's legs to fondle his balls and stroke the taint behind them. Seth jerked beneath him, cried out Evan's name, and came in a rush. Evan swallowed it down, milking Seth's cock with gentle suction until he had taken all his spend, ending with a swipe of his tongue across the knob that made Seth catch his breath.

"Could you tell how grateful I am?" Evan whispered as he stretched up for a kiss so Seth could taste himself on Evan's tongue.

"That was…yes," Seth managed, collapsing bonelessly into the chair. "And…I should thank you for making the pasta. Just to be fair."

Evan stood and shucked off his jeans and briefs, standing so his cock was level with Seth's mouth. "I won't turn down an offer like that," he joked, then gave a very manly yelp as Seth grabbed his ass cheeks and pulled Evan forward to fuck his mouth.

Teasing Seth made Evan hard and wet, and he knew he wouldn't last long, not with the way his lover was going down on him like he was starving for cock. It only took a few bobs of Seth's head before Evan spilled, one hand tight on Seth's shoulder to steady himself, the other in his spiked blond hair. The only sound was Evan's harsh panting. Seth's grip on his ass was all that was keeping Evan on his feet since his knees had turned to jelly.

"We should thank each other more often," Evan said when

his brain could process words again. He leaned down to kiss the top of Seth's head. Seth released him, and Evan smiled.

"What?"

"I bet you left fingerprints," Evan replied. "I like seeing that in the mirror."

"Like being owned?"

"By you? Yes. And it's sexy as fuck when I see mine on you."

"Kinky." Seth tucked Evan away and zipped his fly. "Now I need another shower."

"Hmm. So do I. We could go for a three-fer morning," Evan said with a grin. "I think I like working from home."

THE ELLISON HOUSE WAS A FEDERAL-STYLE BRICK MANSION SET back a long drive lined with an allée of live oak trees. The stately manor looked imposing even in daylight, and Evan shifted uncomfortably as he looked up at the three-story building, feeling like he'd drawn the gaze of a judgmental old man. A window on the second floor was still boarded up, and he guessed it was where the unfortunate husband had been tossed out on his ass.

"You've got the papers, in case someone calls the cops?" he asked.

Seth patted his jacket over the inner pocket. "Right here. On letterhead from the bank. Official permission to do a 'security sweep and analysis,'" he said with a smirk.

"You think Jenner cares what time of day it is?" Evan asked. He had read over all the research for the haunting. The most likely culprit for the aggressive ghost was Jenner Ellison, the owner of the home in the 1950s. From his photograph, Jenner didn't look like he was easy-going about anything in life, so perhaps it was inevitable he'd be tightly wound after death.

"Not according to the witness statements," Seth replied. "He seems to have shown up whenever he pleased. Which sucks for us."

That meant there was no "safe" time to investigate. "He didn't seem to be trying to kill anyone for most of the past sixty-some years. Why now?"

"It's been a private home until the new owners bought it," Seth said as he got out the key the bank rep gave him. "Sometimes that riles up spirits because they feel like they're being invaded. Or, it might be because they acquired some heirlooms from the Ellison family and brought them into the house. I wish people knew how often spirits cling to old possessions. Skip the haunted antiques: buy a good reproduction. I've got a contact down in Charleston, that's their main business—getting cursed and haunted old stuff out of circulation."

Evan had an iron knife in one hand, and a rebar rod in the other. "I feel like I'm going to a gang fight," he muttered. "And I thought iron knives got upgraded in the Bronze Age."

"Maybe for fighting *people*. Iron and salt disrupt ghosts' energy." Hence the salt crystals and iron filings that filled their pockets, and the large container of salt in Seth's bag.

Seth unlocked the door, put the key in his pocket, and took out a small box with a row of lights and an antenna. He'd already explained to Evan how the scanner picked up on the electromagnetic frequencies ghosts gave off. Seth had the meter in one hand and a Ka-Bar with a specially-made high iron-content blade in the other. The EMF reader ticked up immediately when they stepped close to the door, lighting up several of the indicators and giving a quiet, high pitched whine.

"Definitely something here," Seth said as they entered. The formal entranceway had cherry wainscoting up to a chair rail at waist height, and expensive-looking wallpaper with a subtle brown and gold pattern above that. In front of them lay the grand stairway, leading to a second-floor balcony.

"And here I'd been thinking Jenner might have gone on vacation," Evan replied, hoping Seth wouldn't see that his hands shook, just a little.

"No such luck." Seth looked up the stairs. "Let's start on the second floor. If I understood correctly, none of those rooms are completely refinished. Three of the four down here are. Maybe Jenner liked his bedroom the way it was. Stay clear of the windows," he added.

The upstairs smelled of spackle, primer, and sawdust. The workers' tools lay where they had been tossed aside, presumably when the men ran for their lives. Drop cloths covered the floor, and blue painter's tape protected the wood trim.

Seth headed first to the bedroom where the unlucky co-owner had been thrown from the large bay window. Plywood covering the broken glass in the center made the room darker, and Evan shied away from the shadows.

Unexpectedly, the meter stopped squealing, and the sensor's lights blinked off. "What the fuck?" Seth muttered. He shook the box, but the reading didn't change. "I guess Jenner's playing hide-and-seek today," he said. The other three rooms—also in various phases of renovation—were equally quiet.

Seth looked at Evan and shrugged. "If there was something about these rooms anchoring Jenner to the house, it should register on the meter. And there aren't any furnishings or decorations up here right now, so those aren't the anchor. Apparently, he can move around, and he's not feeling sleepy." He walked back to the hallway. "Keep a hand on the railing. Taking a tumble down those stairs wouldn't end well."

Evan sheathed his knife so he could hang on to the balustrade, keeping the rebar in a white-knuckled grip. They moved slowly and carefully, and Evan let out a sigh of relief when they reached the first floor without anything trying to kill them. The two men walked to the front door and then turned around to start their downstairs sweep. The meter perked up, that same low squeal they had heard when they first entered, and several indicator lights lit, flickering on and off, a warning that Jenner was, indeed, at home.

On Evan's left was a room that might be a parlor. The renovations had been interrupted, in the middle of stripping and re-staining the wood paneling. On the right, the already refurbished dining room boasted a large mahogany table that might have been from the 1800s, with eight high-backed chairs and a tall cabinet for storing china.

Seth stepped into the parlor. The EMF meter's reading didn't beep. "Nothing here," he said.

The meter whined when he walked into the dining room but went silent again right away. Evan felt his stomach tighten with fear. The hair on the back of his neck prickled, and he tightened his grip on his weapons, resolved not to be surprised if something popped out in front of him.

Behind the dining room was an office, with painted walls and a modern desk, chair, and filing cabinet that suggested the new owners intended to make it their headquarters. Evan expected the meter to go off, figuring that Jenner would have seen the room as ground zero of the unwanted invasion, but the lights remained unchanged. Seth crossed the hall to the sitting room, and the meter let out a squeal that made Evan jump.

"Found something," Seth muttered, rather redundantly. He stepped in front, leading the way, and holding his Ka-Bar at the ready. Evan followed, protecting Seth as he had promised.

Back in the day, Evan guessed that what was now the office might have done double duty as a men's smoking room, leaving this fourth room for the women to sew or read. It had been remodeled to something approximating its original style, with a rocking chair, an uncomfortable-looking sofa, and floral patterned wallpaper that had a jungle feel to it. In one corner was an ornate birdcage on a stand, next to a Victrola with a huge copper sounding trumpet that reminded Evan of a morning glory bloom. Wedgewood tile bordered a fireplace, and above the mantle hung a large oil painting of a man with stern features, bounded by an elaborate gold frame. The window was stained glass, picking up the garden theme, sending streaks of red, gold, and green into the dusty air.

"Stay close," Seth warned as the meter went wild. The temperature in the room plummeted, and gooseflesh rose on Evan's arms.

Seth pocketed the meter and drew a second knife from a scabbard on his belt. Out in the field, Evan knew he'd have had a shotgun with salt-and-iron-filled shells, but the owners and the bank weren't going to appreciate him shooting up the place. They did have a sawed-off in the bag—with shells filled with table salt—which would affect a ghost, if necessary, without putting too many holes in the woodwork.

Behind them, in the empty entranceway, came the crash of broken glass. Evan turned, but the windows around the doorway were still intact. A cold breeze swept past him, ruffling his hair and making him shiver with dread. Jenner and the house were getting to him. He screwed up his courage, tightened his grip on the knife and rebar, and clenched his jaw, refusing to let the old man win.

Seth stood in the middle of the room, taking a step toward each corner in turn and seeing how the meter reacted. Evan stayed alert, and he had the oppressive sense of being watched. Jenner was present with them; Evan was certain although he could not see an apparition. He couldn't decide whether he was disappointed or relieved not to get an honest-to-god sighting.

"I think it's the painting," Seth whispered as if the old man's spirit might be hard of hearing. "She said it was one of the newer pieces."

Evan saw Seth's gaze flicker from the oil painting to the fireplace. He knew Seth had a lighter in his pocket, and the old canvas would probably go up like tinder. Seth took a step toward the mantle, and Evan moved to cover him.

Jenner Ellison picked that moment to go full frontal, showing up in all his ghostly glory, looking almost solid though, thankfully, completely clothed. He looked a decade older than his younger self in the portrait, with a contemptuous sneer and a murderous gleam in his eyes.

Seth dove toward the painting.

Jenner ran toward Seth, then suddenly vanished.

"Where'd he—" Evan started.

Icy spectral hands gripped his shoulders and hauled him off his feet, hurling him toward the big stained glass window. Evan cried out, part warning, part fear, and flailed wildly. His motion shifted his course but did nothing to slow his momentum. He missed the window, hitting the wall instead, smacking his head hard against the solid wooden frame. Evan tasted blood as his teeth clacked together. Pain exploded behind his eyes. His legs gave way, and he slid down the wall, but he was out cold before he hit the floor.

2

SETH

"Evan!" Seth shouted when he saw his partner tossed across the room like a rag doll. The soldier in him stayed on target. He reached the fireplace and dumped salt and iron filings in a messy circle beneath his feet and around him to keep Jenner at bay.

Come on. Get up, Seth willed for Evan to say something, give him a sign that he was okay. The silence fueled his fears and stoked his rage. Cold wind swirled around him, trying to blow away the salt, but the grains sank into the Aubusson area rug, remaining largely in place.

Jenner Ellison appeared, just on the other side of the protective salt. His eyes held a mad glint, and his lips drew back to bare his teeth as he reached toward Seth with gnarled, clawed hands. Seth ducked and came up with the sawed-off, firing a shell through the ghost's chest to the floor directly behind him. A spray of salt doused the revenant, which shrieked and vanished. Seth was too worried about Evan, too focused on his task, to give a damn about the damage to the hardwoods now.

Seth tore the oil painting down from its place and ripped his knife through the canvas. Then he broke the frame across his thigh until the pieces would fit into the fireplace. He threw the whole jumble in—torn canvas and splintered frame—and squirted it with lighter fluid, then tossed in a couple of lit matches.

"Fuck you, Jenner!" he yelled at the empty room as flames darkened and curled the old painting. A bloodcurdling scream echoed through the house, sounding like it came from everywhere at once. The portrait fell to ash and embers as the varnish and paint on the wooden frame caught like kindling, fueling a blaze that leaped high toward the flue.

Evan. Seth kept the sawed off and his knife in hand as he left the salt circle and ran to where Evan lay against the wall, far too still. "Evan?" he called, trying not to sound as panicked as he felt.

"Evan? Come on, don't check out on me," he said, speaking aloud partly to wake his partner, and partly to calm the frantic pounding of his own heart. He reached for Evan, and his hand came away bloody from a gash on the back of his lover's head where Evan had hit the carved molding, hard.

"Aw, shit," Seth muttered, easing Evan down to lie flat on the floor. He glanced nervously out the window, in case someone had heard the shot and called the cops. Seth felt for a pulse, relaxing just a bit when he felt a steady throb beneath his fingertips, reassuring himself by watching the rise and fall of Evan's chest.

Seth knew they really shouldn't leave until the fire burned out, although sirens would change his plans very quickly. Most of the frame and painting were already gone, leaving charred bits and glowing embers. He left Evan's side just long enough to dump some salt and iron filings onto the ashes, and stirred the mess with a poker, making sure no large pieces remained.

Seconds later, he was back with Evan, gently checking for

broken bones. Evan groaned, and Seth reached to take his hand. "How do you feel?" Seth asked.

"Like I got thrown against a wall," Evan managed. "God, my head hurts."

"Open your eyes," Seth ordered. Evan struggled to comply, and Seth checked his pupils. "I don't think you're concussed, but you're bleeding, and you'll have one hell of a goose egg," he said. "If I help, do you think you can walk? We need to get out of here."

"The bank letter—"

"Cops tend to go all Rambo on you first, and ask questions later," Seth replied, getting to his feet and leaning down to help get Evan. "I might not get the chance to show them the letter before we've cooled our heels for a few hours in a cell. Would rather avoid that, to be honest."

It had only happened once, Seth thought, but that was enough to make him cautious. Milo and Toby had shared plenty of warnings about hunters who did jail time for having been caught at the scene after saving the world, and Seth didn't want to add prison to his resume.

"Yeah. Me, too," Evan replied, wincing as he leaned on Seth. A glance confirmed that the fire had burned completely down, so Seth helped Evan hobble to the door and locked it behind them. This was one time he was glad they had driven the truck instead of the Hayabusa. He loaded Evan into the passenger seat, put a clean towel behind his head to keep the blood off the upholstery, and gave him a once-over. A little pale, blood still seeping from the scalp wound— gonna be black and blue from shoulders to ass most likely—but still breathing and no broken bones.

"No puking in the truck," Seth warned. "I love you, but throwing up in the truck would severely test my affection," he teased.

"Got it," Evan mumbled. "Now drive. Don't want to get arrested. I don't look good in orange."

Seth grinned, relieved that Evan was coherent enough to joke, and went around the front of the truck to climb into the driver's seat. "You? What about me?"

Evan closed his eyes, but he gave a wan smile. "Tat up your knuckles, shave your hair, and you'll look too badass for anyone to cross."

Evan looked sleepy. "No, no, no. Stay awake!" Seth ordered. "Shit. We need to make sure you're okay."

"I'm tired," Evan murmured.

"You can rest in a bit," Seth offered, taking on the tone he used when his younger brother was small and needed to be talked into something. "Just stay with me for a bit."

"Planning to stay," Evan said groggily. Seth's heart did a little flip, not sure whether Evan had spoken a larger truth with his filters down.

"Good," Seth said. "That's real good." He drove back to the campground and helped Evan out of the truck and into the sun. He squinted, ducking his head from the bright light. Seth caught his breath at the dried blood matting Evan's hair and staining the towel.

He could have gotten killed. I didn't prepare him enough. This is all my fault, Seth thought as his gut soured with guilt. He led Evan to a place where the light was good but not glaring.

"Let me have a look," Seth said gently. Evan flinched as Seth carefully lifted the stiffened hair to examine the cut beneath. Seth let out a breath he didn't realize he had been holding when he realized that the gash wouldn't need stitches.

"Bet it hurts like a son of a bitch," Seth commiserated. "But it could have been worse. Probably gonna give you a knot. I'll go for ice."

"Want to sleep."

Seth pulled a small flashlight from his glovebox. "Gotta look at your eyes. See if you're concussed," he said apologetically. He remembered doing field triage back in the army, trying to figure out who needed a medic, stat. Evan winced but stayed still as Seth checked his eyes, and was relieved to find them normal.

"What's your name? Who am I? What year is this?"

Evan made a face and answered all three questions with waning patience. "Now will you let me fucking lie down?"

Seth gave a relieved laugh. "If you're well enough to cuss me out, you're probably okay. How about if you lie down while I get ice, and then I'll close us up and get us ready for the road."

"We're leaving?" Evan sounded like a sleepy kid, and Seth's heart squeezed a little.

"We got rid of the ghost, but I'm not sure how my bank client is going to feel about the damage I did to the floor, or about us destroying the painting."

"M'sorry," Evan mumbled, looking contrite.

"Not your fault," Seth said in a firm voice. "That asshole Jenner hurt you, and I was going to put him down." He cleared his throat. "But I thought, just to be safe, we'd better check out here and pull up stakes, get on the road before I call the client and tell him."

"Okay," Evan replied. "Bed?"

Seth chuckled. "Just for you, right now. Until you feel better."

"Didn't get hit in the nuts," Evan grumbled.

"Glad to hear it," Seth replied. "But I doubt making your heart pound right now would do good things to your head."

"Depends on which head." Evan smiled, just a little, and Seth figured if he could even consider sex, he was probably not quite at death's door.

"Tonight, I promise. If you feel up to it. Once we're hell and gone from here," Seth said, adjusting himself a bit at the thought. He'd never turned down a proposition from Evan, but he knew that all the good endorphins from pounding one end would cause an unpleasant throbbing at the other end.

"Okay," Evan accepted, sleepy and sulky. Seth helped him up the three stairs into the fifth wheeler and then led him to the dining area.

"Let's get you cleaned up and out of those bloody clothes," he said with a sigh. He wanted to hit the road before trouble could find them, but Evan looked like he'd been mugged, which would bring other, unwanted questions. Not to mention get blood on the sheets.

"This way, Sleeping Beauty," Seth coaxed, maneuvering Evan to a seat. Evan flipped him the bird.

"Fuck you," Evan said without heat.

"I already promised you could," Seth chuckled. He dodged into the bedroom and came out with a pair of jeans and a fresh shirt. Evan had lost everything in the apartment fire, and there had only been time since then to pick up a few necessities. He felt a pang of guilt. *I'm not taking very good care of him. Shit. I've got to do better.* He grabbed a dark towel from the small bathroom on his way back.

"Let me get the worst of the gunk out of your hair," he said when he returned to the kitchen and grabbed a pair of latex gloves from under the sink. Seth ran the towel under warm water, and carefully wiped off the blood from Evan's face and neck.

"That's better," he said and moved around to the back. "This might sting, but it'll be worse if we let it dry."

Seth rinsed blood out of the hand towel several times, gently wiping at the matted hair, and assuring himself that the wound would close on its own. Evan bore the prodding stoically, although his fists closed, white-knuckled, from time to time. Finally, Seth figured he'd gotten out the worst, and the rest would wash out in the shower. He stripped out of the gloves, tossed them in the trash, and grabbed an ice pack from the freezer. When Evan stood, Seth watched to make sure he looked steady on his feet.

"Let's get you into bed," Seth said, steering him toward

the bedroom and making sure he didn't trip on the few steps up.

"Don't want to go alone."

Apparently, an injured Evan was a little clingy. Seth grinned and wondered how much his partner would remember. "I'm coming with you to get you settled. Then I have to get us out of here, so we don't get in trouble."

Evan mumbled something that might have been agreement.

"Sit on the edge, and I'll take your shoes off. You don't want to bend over, or your head will throb. Trust me on that," Seth warned, having taken a few good hits himself over the years.

He got down to unlace Evan's boots. Evan ran a hand through Seth's hair. "I like you like that," Evan said quietly, as Seth knelt between his legs.

Seth willed his hard-on to settle. *Down, boy. Not getting any for a while.* "I like being here," Seth replied as he gently untangled Evan's hand and stood. With one hand behind Evan's shoulders, he used the other hand to flip his legs up and then gentled him down.

"This is your side," Evan protested.

"It's just a nap," Seth said. "You can't ride in the trailer when we're moving. I'll get things ready and then come back to wake you up and bring you out to the truck. You want to ride with me, right?"

Evan's eyes were shut, but he managed a tired leer. "I always want to ride you."

"Glad to know there's no injury to your downstairs brain, at least," Seth said, surprising himself at how fond his tone sounded. "Stay put. I don't want you to fall on the steps if you get wobbly."

"Bossy," Evan said, barely above a whisper.

Seth stood in the doorway as Evan relaxed into sleep,

watching him breathe. Now that the emergency was over, he felt his own emotions hit him with full force.

Shit. I could have gotten him killed. This is why guys like me hunt alone. But then he thought of Toby and Milo, together for decades. And about his friend Simon, a clairvoyant medium and folklore expert, who was finding his way in a new relationship with his skeptical cop boyfriend, Vic.

Am I selfish to want him to stay, when he'd be so much safer away from me? Seth wondered. Then again, he wasn't entirely sure about that. He and Milo had worked out a theory that the witch-disciples of dark warlock Rhyfel Gremory each chose a victim from one of the families of the deputies who killed Gremory every dozen years. Evan had been marked for death by Corson Valac, whom they'd destroyed. But did that mean another of the witch-disciples couldn't get an extra "power boost" by killing their chosen descendant and Evan, too?

Maybe, despite the dangers of their "side gig," Evan really would be safer here where Seth could protect him. *Great job I've done so far*, Seth castigated himself. *Am I making excuses?* The truth was, just the thought of leaving Evan behind made Seth feel sick.

He reminded himself that he had other things to do, other ways to keep Evan safe that started with getting them out of town. With a final, lingering look, Seth headed outside.

Before he started closing down the water, sewage, and electrical hook-ups and reconnecting the trailer to his Silverado, Seth figured he owed Milo and Toby a call. Milo answered on the third ring.

"How'd it go? You get him?" Milo asked.

Seth scrubbed a hand down over his face, suddenly exhausted. "Yeah. Ganked the ghost, but he went after Evan before I could stop him. Threw him into the wall."

Milo was quiet for longer than Seth expected. "He okay?"

"Yeah, yeah. Just banged up. Scalp wound, nothing too

bad. He's resting in the trailer. I'm not sure the client's going to be happy that I damaged his floor and burned a painting."

He could almost hear Milo shrug. "The property was useless with the ghost active, perfect floor or not."

"Guess we'll see what he thinks."

"You haven't called the bank guy?"

Seth winced. "I figured we'll get on the road first. Just in case."

"Eh. Not a bad strategy," Milo agreed. "So how are you doing? First hunt with Evan after the witch-disciple and all."

Shit. Milo had him dead to rights. Seth stepped away from the trailer to lean on a utility shed. "He got hurt. I didn't protect him. Maybe…" He didn't want to put his fear into words.

"Did Toby ever tell you how we got together?" Milo asked. In the background, Seth could hear Toby yelling something, and Milo returned a good-natured "shut up" to his partner.

"No, but I get the feeling you're going to."

"Damn right," Milo replied. "I was a rookie cop. First week on the job. Completely wet behind the ears. I saw a truck parked out by an abandoned farm, and decided it was my duty to investigate."

"Let me guess—"

"You gonna let me tell this story or not?"

Seth sighed. "Go on."

"As I was saying," Milo went on, clearing his throat for emphasis, although Seth was almost certain his mentor was smiling, "I go in there, thinking I'm probably bustin' up some teenagers drinking, maybe some druggies. But before I even reach the porch, something fast and strong tackles me from behind. I walked into a ghoul nest."

Seth thought of several smart comments and decided to keep his mouth shut.

"That thing had me, and he would have finished me, too,

except all of a sudden, I hear a shot, and the ghoul's head explodes all over me. I look up, and there are four of them, all around me. And this big, broad-shouldered hunk is standing over me, protecting me, and he just pops them, bang, bang, bang, bang."

Despite himself, Seth wondered where the story was going.

"He gets me up and tells me to get out of there, that it's not my kind of thing," Milo recalled, chuckling fondly. "I was green, but I realized fast that those things weren't human. And then, Toby just keels over." Muted but vehement protest sounded from somewhere behind Milo.

"You did too," Milo argued with his husband. He returned to the call with a long-suffering, exaggerated sigh. "Any-way...turns out he'd gotten clawed up real good. So he tells me how to burn the bodies, and I have this choice, you know? Trust this guy I've never seen before who just saved my life from things that look like they walked out of a horror movie, or call it in like I'm supposed to do."

Milo paused, but before Seth could jump in, he went on. "I went with my gut. Burned the ghouls, and loaded the guy into his truck and drove him to his motel, since I could hardly put him in the police car. He wouldn't let me take him to the hospital, so I patched him up with the kit he had, gave him some whiskey, and realized the poor bastard had a fever."

"So there I was. I'd left my cruiser back at the scene. Broke a bunch of rules—not to mention, laws—with all the shooting and burning, and I was aiding and abetting. I'd have been lucky if I just lost my badge."

"Why'd you do it?" Seth asked,

"Thirty-five years later, I can't really explain it," Milo replied. "Except, I just knew in my gut that if I let this guy go, I'd regret it for the rest of my life. So...I sat up with him all night until the fever broke. Went and got him breakfast, and we talked. He told me about what he hunted. I realized that I wanted to do that more than bust beer parties and give out traffic tickets. I told him I intended to come with him."

"And he took you? Just like that?"

Milo barked a laugh. "Oh, hell no! He turned me down flat. Then I told him that I either came with him or I'd arrest him on the spot and drag him to jail."

"I bet that went over well."

"He took me with him—and promptly tried to dump my ass at a rest stop," Milo recounted. Toby's protests in the background had gotten louder, and included more profanity. "I found him down the road a piece, and he did it again —twice."

"How did you find him?" Seth asked, barely able to contain his laughter.

"I'm stubborn—and a damned good tracker," Milo confessed. "By that point, I guess he decided that it was easier to just take me along. We got involved pretty soon after that, and, well, it's been thirty-five years." He paused. "I'm just saying, don't rule something out because of the life you lead. It can work—with the right two people."

God, Seth hoped Milo was right about that. Seth had never felt about anyone the way he did for Evan. He'd given up hope that there might be a relationship out there for him, after the betrayals in his past. But Evan…Evan made him feel alive and a little giddy, vulnerable, and protective—and so many other things, all at once. It was an overwhelming, wonderful rush, and Seth hoped it never ended.

"Wouldn't hurt you to give him more training than you've probably had time to do." The voice was Toby's now, apparently having wrested the phone away from Milo. "I taught Milo things I learned in the war to keep him safe," he added, and Seth knew Toby meant 'Nam. "Spar. Show him how to use the weapons. Teach him a bit of rote magic. Give him what he needs to protect himself—and you."

Seth humphed. "Yeah. You're right. We've covered some of that, but shit, there just hasn't been a lot of time—"

"Make time," Toby ordered. "You hear me?"

"I hear you," Seth echoed. "And before I start hearing sirens, I'd better haul ass. I'll let you know where we hole up."

"Yeah. Do that. And I've got feelers out for anything we can find out about the Pittsburgh situation. I'll let you know when I've got something," Toby said and ended the call.

Seth pushed away from the shed and went to the camp office to pay up. The office was in a corner of the big social room and concession stand that was probably a hot spot all summer long. Now, in early November, it seemed lonely and deserted. The huge TV was tuned to a channel with 1970s sitcom re-runs, but the tables and chairs were all empty, and both the convenience store and the concession stand were closed. A sign redirected out-of-season campers to the vending machines and gave a list of pizza joints that delivered to the campgrounds.

"Mrs. M?" Seth called out. Aggie MacArthur poked her head out of the office door.

"Oh, hello Seth. Something I can do for you?" With her short, graying hair and trim figure, Aggie looked like she probably embraced the outdoor life herself when she wasn't running the campgrounds with her husband, Tom. It didn't take much imagination to picture her guiding a kayak through whitewater or climbing boulders.

"I need to pay you and let you know we're moving on," Seth said, hoping he didn't look nervous. "Thanks for having us. The campground is great."

"Sorry that you're heading out so soon," she said, motioning for him to come to the office doorway. There really wasn't room for him inside; Aggie's chair, desk, and beat-up metal filing cabinet were squeezed in so tightly Seth wondered how she managed to get into her seat. "I hope there wasn't a problem with your spot?" She laughed. "This time of year, you pretty much have your pick of other sites if that one didn't suit."

"Oh no," Seth hurried to assure her. "Nothing like that. We just promised friends we'd meet them up north and we need to get going, so we aren't late." It wasn't exactly a lie, although it also wasn't precisely the truth.

"Well, if you ever pass by this way again, you're always welcome," Aggie said, counting out the cash Seth gave her and handing him a receipt. He had credit cards, but they left a trail. If they wanted to be able to move without being easily traced, they paid cash.

"I'll keep that in mind," Seth replied. Most of the time, the people who ran the campgrounds or the occasional motel made no attempt to forge even a superficial personal connection. Saving the world was a lonely business. People like Aggie—even if Seth never saw her again—made it bearable.

And now, I've got Evan. If he stays.

Seth headed back to the RV. He'd gotten good at hooking the truck up to the fifth-wheeler in just minutes, something he'd practiced for times when a quick getaway was essential. He double-checked the hitch, made sure the power cord and breakaway switch cable were connected and tossed the wheel blocks into the storage area beneath the trailer after he raised the landing gear and closed the tailgate. Then he went inside to rouse Evan.

The bed was empty.

"Evan? Evan!" Seth shouted. No one in the bathroom; nobody in the kitchen. The bed was still mussed from where Evan napped, but his shoes were gone. *What the hell?*

Seth ran back outside. "Evan!" he yelled. The wind seemed to catch his words and carry them away.

He stood, hands on hips, and turned in a circle. Evan hadn't come looking for him in the rec room. The arcade was closed. With only a few other trailers in the park, Seth could see from one end almost to the other. He walked to the opposite side of the fifth-wheeler, looking down the slope toward the camp's basketball court, mini-golf course, and duck pond. There, seated on the bench overlooking the water, was Evan.

With a sigh of relief, Seth jogged down and dropped onto the bench beside Evan. "You scared the shit out of me. I didn't know where you'd gone."

Evan shrugged. "Sorry. You said we were leaving, and I wanted to come down here to see the ducks and geese again before we went." In one hand, he held a bread bag with stale end crusts. He ripped off a piece of bread and tossed it toward the birds at the edge of the water. "I used to like to feed the squirrels in the park in front of the State House, back in Richmond," Evan said, his attention on the birds as they gobbled down the bread. He didn't sound self-conscious, but then again, he didn't look directly at Seth as he spoke, either.

"My mom used to take Jesse and me to the park when we were little," Seth said, figuring that they could wait until the bread was gone. "We'd throw bread to the ducks and geese, and pellets to the fish in the lake. And then one time, a big goose started chasing Jesse because he ran out of bread. I started flapping my arms and yelling to draw the goose off, and Jesse pretty much climbed my mom to get away." He chuckled, but the memory was bittersweet now that Jesse was gone. He inched closer to Evan and slipped an arm around his shoulders. Evan leaned in, resting his head against him.

"There were always squirrels in the backyard when I was a kid," Evan replied. "I used to love putting out peanuts for them, but my mom made me stop because she thought the squirrels would get into the attic." Evan hadn't seen his parents in years, not since they'd taken his coming out badly.

"Why don't you finish up with the geese, and wherever we end up staying, we'll go looking for a park with squirrels?" Seth promised and leaned down to kiss the top of his head. "We'd better get going."

"I know," Evan said. He stood, and they walked down together toward the edge of the pond, tossing out torn bits of bread that had the ducks and geese in a flurry, fighting for the spoils. When the hungry birds turned their beady eyes on their now-empty-handed donors, Seth and Evan made a beeline for the RV.

"Where are we heading?" Evan asked once they were on the road.

"Beckley, West Virginia," Seth replied. "There's another campground there that's open this season. Free Wi-Fi, trailer hookups, and a little diner next door that does pretty awesome breakfasts and burgers."

"Sounds like a plan," Evan said. He closed his eyes and slouched against the door, giving Seth to guess that he was still feeling the aftereffects of the fight.

"One of the things I like about the campground in Beckley is that it's got plenty of room to train," Seth broached the subject. "Once you feel better, we need to ramp up the sparring, and get you up-to-speed with the lore and weapons."

Evan didn't open his eyes. "You talked to Milo and Toby, didn't you?"

Seth sighed. "Yeah, but I'd already figured I needed to make sure you could hold your own in a fight. Show you some rote spells, too."

"I'd like that," Evan said, but his voice was still frayed with pain. "Whatever it takes. I'm not going anywhere without you," he promised before soft snoring assured Seth that his partner had fallen back asleep.

A WEEK LATER, EVAN SAT AT THE TABLE IN THE RV WITH PAPERS spread in every direction. Between Evan's need to recuperate and days of rain, they hadn't stepped up his physical training beyond what they could do indoors, which included learning to throw knives at the dart board. When Evan tired, Seth drilled him on sigils and protective plants.

"I feel like I'm studying for finals," Evan said, pushing a stray lock of hair behind his ear. "Or competing on the weirdest gameshow, ever. I'll take 'how to banish demons for $500, Alex,'" he said, doing his best Jeopardy impression.

Seth grinned and stepped closer, running his fingertips gently across Evan's jawline. "This is much better than a gameshow," he said, dropping his voice into a sexy growl. "Every time you get all the answers right in a category, I get you off. Get the whole slate right, and we quit early and fuck like rabbits."

Evan's tongue darted out to slide along Seth's fingers. "And we weren't going to boink like bunnies anyhow?"

"Extra credit sex is different," Seth teased. "You know, hot for teacher?"

"You know how to motivate a student," Evan replied, flecks of gold flashing in his brown eyes as he licked a stripe down Seth's index finger, in a very good imitation of what Seth wanted him to do somewhere else.

"Don't think you've managed to distract me," Seth said, although he sounded a little more breathy than stern. "One more time through drawing the sigils, and one more page of magical plants...then we can have recess," he promised, with a suggestive waggle of eyebrows.

"I don't know—if I'm bad, will you spank me?" Evan asked with a dirty grin.

As if Seth's prick hadn't been hard enough. He stepped back, reluctantly. Teasing aside, he needed to get Evan up to speed. "Maybe. But I'm more worried about having a monster whip your ass. So...answers first, and playtime later."

Evan turned back to his notes with an exaggerated sigh. Still, Seth noted that with practice, Evan's drawings had become much faster and more precise, and he had a good memory for the many plants, herbs, and roots used to ward off evil, work a conjuring, or make a healing poultice.

"It's not supposed to rain tomorrow," Seth said when they finally finished up and put the paperwork away. "We can get in some knife skills practice out in the backfield, and I found a shooting range where we can let you try different types of guns and see what suits you."

Seth expected a smart or lascivious comment on that last remark, but Evan looked surprisingly serious. "Yeah. I mean, I grew up in the country. I can handle a rifle and a shotgun. My grandpa taught me." Evan's voice grew sad, as it always did when he mentioned his estranged family. "But we never had handguns around. Wasn't really a need for them."

"The better you are with one, the better our chances," Seth said, leaning back against the wall and folding his arms over his chest. The day was overcast and cold, with rain streaking down the windows and threatening snow. The electric fireplace gave a cheery glow and welcome warmth.

Evan turned to look out the window at the rain-blurred landscape. "My boss gave me a gun when Mike was stalking me. I really thought he'd kill me if he caught up to me. Still not convinced he wouldn't try."

Evan's old boyfriend hadn't been willing to let go. Seth was grateful that so far, his path hadn't crossed with Mike's because he knew it would be trouble.

"All the more reason to be able to defend yourself," Seth said, tamping down on the protective anger that rose every time he thought about Evan's stalker. "If you can hold your own with the kinds of creatures we'll hunt between witch-disciples, one crazy-ass ex isn't going to seem so scary." He paused. "And, you've got me now. I'm not going to let anybody hurt you."

Jesus, he hoped he could keep that promise.

If the guy at the indoor shooting range desk wondered whether Seth and Evan were friends or more, he kept his opinions to himself, although he followed them with his gaze as they looked around the waiting area. Seth kept up a running commentary in a voice pitched just for Evan as they looked at photos of the guns available to shoot. Some, Seth had used in the military, while others were now part of his hunting arsenal.

"If we took on an army of liches or zombies, an AR-15 might come in handy, but for most of the things we're likely to run into, it's overkill, and the ammo is expensive," Seth said. "And I hate to disappoint you if you've got your heart set on a Desert Eagle like in all those action movies, but it's heavy and not real reliable."

He steered Evan toward another set of pictures. "You can pick whatever you want to try, but I'd suggest a Colt 1911, a Glock, and a Sig Sauer. Good, reliable guns that are real work-horses and aren't easy to break."

A man with a shaved head walked toward them. Seth took one look and figured him for ex-military. From the once-over the guy gave him, Seth guessed the appraisal was mutual.

"Seth and Evan?" Mitch, the instructor, greeted them. He extended his hand to Seth first and shook with a firm grip. "What brings you out tonight?"

"Self-defense," Evan replied, looking both resolute and vulnerable. "Seth wants me to know how to protect myself when he's not home."

If Mitch had wondered whether they were *together*, that made it clear enough. To his credit, the instructor didn't bat an eye. "Of course. That makes sense." He turned to Seth. "Where did you serve?" he asked, without bothering to ask "if" Seth had been in the military.

"Iraq. Army. You?"

"Marines. Afghanistan. *Semper Fi.*"

Seth was long past pissing matches between the branches and let the comment go. "We're in the market for a good gun for him, but I want to make sure he's comfortable with the weight and the recoil, and that the grip fits." He held up a large hand and splayed his fingers. "What works for me isn't necessarily going to work for him."

"Of course," Mitch replied, warming to the subject. "Show me what you want to try, and then we'll go to the range."

They picked out the three handguns Seth preferred, and Mitch suggested that Evan also try a Beretta and a Smith & Wesson. Then they grabbed their protective headsets and followed Mitch out to the range. Seth hung back as the instructor ran through the safety rules. Evan listened carefully, asking questions now and again, much more into the lesson that Seth had expected. When Evan finally took the Colt, he held it firmly, with a natural stance that confirmed that he had handled a gun before. He might not have a lot of experience, but he wasn't afraid of a firearm.

Evan's first round hit center mass every shot, though not always heart-zone. Still, not bad for however long it had been since he had fired a gun. But what intrigued Seth was that Evan raised the gun from his side to sight and shoot in one smooth movement, not using the "Weaver stance" most people were taught.

"How'd you learn to shoot that way?" Seth asked, curious.

Evan blushed. "My grandpa was in World War II. That's how he learned, so that's how he taught me. Said the gun would wobble if I just held it there."

Mitch chuckled. "He's not wrong. That's the way they did it back then, and we won the war, didn't we?" He took a step toward Evan. "Still, if you're in a situation where you have to hold a gun on someone, you might want to at least know the other option. Let me adjust your stance," Mitch said, coming around behind Evan and shifting his body to the different form. Seth was surprised at the sudden flare of jealousy at the sight of Mitch's hands on Evan's shoulders.

Evan tried the rest of the guns in both stances, and his aim improved as the night went on. Seth had no doubt that with regular practice, Evan could do very well. He was used to taking care of himself, but knowing that Evan was protected made Seth feel more confident about bringing him into the hunting life.

We don't have to hunt forever. Just until we destroy all the witch-disciples, and then we can retire, knowing that Evan's safe, Jesse's avenged, and those bastards won't be coming after me or anyone else, ever again.

"I think he's a natural," Mitch said, clapping a meaty hand on Evan's shoulder. "Get him on a range on a regular basis, and I think he'll be just fine."

"Any idea which gun you favor?" Seth asked.

Evan frowned. "I see why you like the Glock. The Sig and the 1911 are nice, but it might make things simpler if we had the same gun."

Mitch walked them out. "Here's a coupon for shooting supplies over at the sporting goods store. They give a discount when you show them your receipt from here. Tell Gus at the gun counter that I sent you," he added with a grin.

Seth and Evan rode back to the campground, watching the wipers clear the rain from the windshield. "So you liked that?" Seth finally asked. He didn't know how it could be possible to feel at once so comfortable with someone and as tongue-tied as a teenager at the prom.

"Yeah," Evan replied. "I want to hold my own in this—all of this," he said. "So the graphic design stuff contributes to the income. And what you're teaching me means I can watch your back."

"You don't fancy being a kept lover?" Seth joked.

Evan gave him a wry look. "No. I like being equals. Always thought that'd be the way it should be if I ever—" he broke off what he was going to say. Seth could guess. From what Evan had told him, his luck with relationships in the past had been bad—and so had Seth's. Neither of them had a lot of experience being a long-time couple. *On the other hand, the scars we've both got are plenty.*

Seth cleared his throat. "I've got a line on a ghoul nest if you think you're up for it. How's your head?"

Evan's hand went to touch the lump on the back of his skull. "Better than it was. But otherwise, I'm fine. So as long as I can keep from getting hit in the same place, I think I'm good to go."

"Milo said he got a call from a buddy of his, Mark Wojcik. Hunter up near Erie. Got a tip about the ghouls, but he doesn't come this far south. Milo figured we were in the area, so he tossed it to us—if, you know, you want to."

"What do I need to know?" Evan asked. The wipers beat a steady rhythm, and the road back to the campgrounds gleamed with the red and white of headlights and tail lights.

"Ghouls are carrion-feeders. They break into graves and eat the dead. If they can't do that, they get by on roadkill. They prefer their food to be decaying, but they'll eat a fresh kill if they're hungry enough. That includes people."

"There went my appetite."

"All the ghouls I've seen are skinny and pale, with knobby joints and big heads and really sharp fingernails," Seth went on. "They're fast, too. Way smarter than zombies. Ghouls *have* brains, they don't *eat* them. So they're wily. And they have teeth like a piranha. If they bite or scratch you, you've got to cleanse the wound and get some antibiotics because it'll get infected fast."

"How do we kill them?" Evan replied, resolute despite everything Seth had said. Seth felt a twinge of pride at that.

"Bullet to the head. Doesn't have to be silver. Whacking off the head works even better. I'll ask Mark who around here sells to hunters. Need to get you a gun and a Ka-Bar, but it's better if they're not traceable."

Evan winced at that. "You know we have to fly under the radar," Seth said. "Like what happened in Richmond—the cops would have had our guts for garters. Some of them know about the creatures out there, but most don't, and they'd toss us in the psych ward if we tried to tell them."

Evan nodded. "I know. It's just, I've only had two speeding tickets. Ever."

Seth bit his lip, drumming his fingers on the wheel. "If you want out, I don't blame you."

Evan turned and fixed him with a glare. "That's not what I mean. I told you—I'm in. It just takes some getting used to." He smirked. "I guess this makes me Bonnie to your Clyde."

"Grow a mustache, and we could do Butch and Sundance."

They fell silent as the truck pulled into the campground. Like the park in Virginia, it was nearly empty given that winter was on its way. Seth suspected that the few trailers left were people who had nowhere else to go.

"When do you want to go after the ghouls?" Evan asked when they parked.

Seth turned to him. The overhead security fixture set Evan's face in a study of light and shadow. He looked determined, a little scared, and fucking beautiful.

"How about tomorrow night? Time we headed north anyhow. I'll pay for us to stay that night, and we'll leave as soon as we're done with the ghouls."

"All right," Evan said with determination. He took a deep breath and squared his shoulders. "All right," he repeated a little quieter, as if to himself. "That works."

They made love slowly that night, savoring the taste and scent of each other, the slide of skin against skin, the slow build to a nearly simultaneous release. Afterward, Seth and Evan lay in the darkness, tangled together, sated and spent. Evan rested his head on Seth's shoulder, and Seth wrapped an arm around him, drawing him close.

How do Milo and Toby deal with the fear? Seth wondered, content to listen to the steady rhythm of Evan's breathing and feel the throb of his pulse. *I didn't really much care before if I got killed, as long as I ended that damn warlock's disciples. But now...I want something "after." I want Evan. So I've got to make sure we both make it out alive.*

The next night was cold and cloudy, but thankfully without rain. They took the Hayabusa, leaving the truck already hitched to the RV for a quick getaway. Evan held on tight, obviously still not comfortable with the wind and the speed of the bike. The duffel slung over Evan's back held their knives and two sawed-off shotguns. They each wore their handguns in back holsters; secure on the ride, easy to conceal.

"This is it?" Evan asked, and if his voice sounded hoarse, Seth pretended not to notice. The abandoned country church had been empty for a long time. Peeling white paint and smashed windows added to the sense of desolation, as did the high brown weeds and the broken steeple. To one side lay an old cemetery, its headstones cracked and leaning.

"Yeah," Seth replied in a voice barely above a whisper. He left the bike down the lane in the shadows beneath a row of trees. They grabbed their weapons and started up the gravel drive together.

"Too bad we can't just torch the place."

Seth gave him the side-eye. "I like how you think. But... that's a last resort. Attracts too much attention. Still, never say never."

He agreed with Evan. Lobbing a Molotov into the old building would minimize their risk. The dry siding would go up like tinder. On the other hand, just burning the place didn't guarantee the ghouls would be in it. Better to do it old school and make sure.

Outside, there was enough moonlight to see fairly well. Seth intended to draw the ghouls out. He had no desire to hunt for the creatures in the abandoned sanctuary, or even worse, the basement. If his plan worked, they wouldn't have to.

"We could split up, each take a side."

"Hell, no. Don't you watch TV? That's never a good idea." Seth and Evan closed in on the church, and Seth looked for the basement windows he had seen in the Google Earth footage he had looked up earlier in the day. "Okay—there it is," he murmured, mostly to himself as he spotted the opening.

"Fire in the hole!" Seth hissed to Evan, warning him to look away and cover his ears. He lobbed a homemade flash-bang grenade through the glass, then pulled Evan down with him to a crouch, their backs to the explosion of light and sound.

Even at a distance, the bright white flare made them see red inside eyelids squeezed tightly shut. Fingers in their ears deadened the worst of the boom but still left Seth with a faint ringing. If the ghouls were in the building, they'd gotten a wake-up call they couldn't ignore.

Shadows shifted at the edge of the cemetery, rapidly growing closer. Seth heard chattering teeth and a strange whining sound. The ghouls weren't in the old church. They'd been in the woods—and now they were headed right for Seth and Evan.

"Shit!" Seth pulled his shotgun, and Evan mirrored his action. Five misshapen figures ran toward them. Even with their features hidden by the darkness, Seth could make out enough in the moonlight to know the creatures weren't human. The heads were too big, the arms hung too long, and the hunched way they ran set off every primal survival instinct Seth had.

Evan widened his stance and fit the shotgun against his shoulder. They waited until there was little chance of missing, and fired together. The front two ghouls fell with an ear-splitting shriek of pain and rage. Seth and Evan fired again. One ghoul fell, but the other shot went wide. They dropped their shotguns and drew their handguns. The last two ghouls spread out, forcing the two hunters to pivot so that they stood back to back.

"Where are they?" Evan breathed. The remaining ghouls had dropped to all fours, hidden in the tall weeds.

"Out there. Wait for it."

The ghoul popped up in front of Seth closer than he thought possible and backhanded him with a fist that sent him sprawling. He heard Evan's shout, then a gunshot, but the ghoul launched himself at Seth, clever enough to pin his gun arm to the ground while the other hand went for Seth's throat.

The next shot sounded so loud and close Seth was certain he'd been hit. Cold ichor and bits of stinking flesh sprayed all over him. The now-headless ghoul remained on its knees for a few seconds, then toppled to one side just as Seth realized that he hadn't taken a bullet himself.

Evan stood silhouetted against the moonlight, his new Glock in hand. "You all right?" he asked in a shaky voice.

Seth pushed up from the ground, scraping ghoul guts off himself and wrinkling his nose at the smell. "Yeah. Well, other than the mess. Thanks."

Evan nodded. "Yeah. Sure. I got the other one while you were fighting the last ghoul off. Is that all of them?"

Seth retrieved their shotguns, keeping a wary eye on the overgrown lawn around them. "If there were any others, they'd have attacked by now. So they either ran off, which isn't likely, or this was it."

"Good. That's...good." Evan sounded a little shocky, but he hadn't lost his nerve and had yet to puke at the sights and smells.

"Come on, Firebug," Seth said with as much humor as he could muster. "Gotta burn the bodies without setting the field on fire. Then I think we're gonna pull into that do-it-yourself car wash we passed on the way in and hose ourselves off before we ride home."

"That works." Evan's tone was a bit mechanical, something Seth recognized from his own first firefight. He helped drag the ghoul bodies to a pile on a bare stretch of ground, then watched as Seth sprinkled the heap with salt and lighter fluid, tossing in a match to set the pyre aflame. Evan stood facing the opposite way, gun in hand, watching Seth's back.

"That's our cue to haul ass," Seth said and grabbed the duffel. He and Evan jogged back to the motorcycle, and if Evan held on a little tighter than usual, Seth wasn't going to mention it.

Later, once they were out of danger, the reality of what happened and what could have happened would hit. And when it did, Seth intended for them to be clean and safe, wrapped up in soft sheets and each other's arms.

3

EVAN

"I'm not sure that I'm cut out to do magic," Evan said, giving a snort of frustration as he held his open palm above an unlit candle that remained...unlit.

"Give yourself time," Seth coached. "You're trying to take in a lot, all at once."

"Because I need to be able to hold my own when we find the next witch-disciple!" Evan argued, feeling out of sorts. He knew it wasn't Seth's fault; in fact, his partner had been remarkably patient with his training. And a month ago, it never would have crossed Evan's mind that he—or anyone— might be able to learn simple spells. The "rote magic" Seth tried to teach him lay in remembering words to help focus his energy and direct it toward a goal, like opening a lock, moving a small object without touching it...or summoning fire to light a candle.

"And you will," Seth encouraged. "Look, I trained for two years before I went out looking for those bastards. I'm sure I wasn't an ideal student—ask Milo and Toby." He chuckled and rubbed his neck. "On second thought..."

Evan pushed the candle away and crossed his arms. "Maybe I'm not the magical type."

Seth grinned. "You're plenty magical in my book." He added an exaggerated leer, and Evan knew his lover was trying to cheer him up.

"Want to play with my wand?"

"Always," Seth replied, dropping to give him a kiss. Before Evan could unfold his arms to get in a quick grope, Seth stepped back. "You know, maybe it's the spells. Just because these were the spells that came fairly easily to me, doesn't mean they will to you." He sat down across the table from Evan and picked up the book Milo had given him.

The old volume didn't look like a spell book to Evan. With its stained and fraying canvas cover, lettering nearly worn unreadable, it more closely resembled a hard-used textbook. And maybe that wasn't entirely inaccurate. Seth had told him that the minor magics were considered "rote" because they required the caster to have the spell memorized. Higher magic by people with real power could apparently be made up on the spot.

"What did you have in mind?" Evan asked, curious despite his failed attempts.

"Nothing too fancy," Seth replied, flipping through pages. "Something practical, or that you can use as a defense. You don't have to go Gandalf on his ass. Just something helpful and unexpected."

Evan tried to think of examples. Seth could unlock a lock, make a small object zip through the air, send a stream of fire several feet. All those bits of rote magic had helped to save Evan's life in the fight against Valac. Evan searched his mind for ideas.

"Could I tell if someone was lying? Sense zombies?"

Seth shrugged. "We can look them up. My friend Simon—the folklore guy—told me that some people believe that the easiest magics to learn are the ones that enhance things you're already good at."

"That's me, the magical mixologist," Evan chuckled, a

reference to his old job. "But if that's the case, then getting people to tell me the truth isn't far off. Everyone talks to the bartender." He thought for a moment. "Drawing those sigils came pretty easy for me. Graphic design, you know? Maybe I'm better drawing spells than saying them."

The sigils Seth had already taught him to draw didn't require any extra magic "juice" from the artist to make them work. The magic was in the pattern, and the short activation phrase that went with it, but could be worked by anyone, regardless of talent or practice. But maybe there were others —advanced marks—that could do more.

So far, he had learned to draw sigils for "light," "silence," and "distract." Drawn on a solid object, the sigils would glow, dampen sound, or make someone look away from that spot. Useful, but not very powerful.

Seth leaned across the table and gave him another kiss. "Beautiful—and brilliant." He rustled a few more old pages. "Look."

The yellowed parchment and faded ink made the arcane patterns look even more mysterious. "There's a 'summon ghosts' sigil that becomes a 'banish ghosts' mark if I put a line through it," Evan mused. "And a 'compel truth' sign. I guess if I cross out that one, the person has to lie?"

"And whaddya know, a 'sense undead' sigil," Seth noted. "I guess all those D&D players didn't make everything up, after all."

"What's the opposite of that one?"

Seth shrugged. "Maybe 'repel'? Not sure I want to try it to find out."

"There's also a 'fasten/release' sigil," Evan pointed out. "That might work like your 'unlock' spell—could be handy for both of us to be able to do."

"Sounds like plenty to start with," Seth said, and Evan returned his smile. Speaking a word spell like Seth did and filling it with his energy seemed awkward, like trying to write with his left hand. But drawing…Evan had always put so much of himself in his sketches that a teacher once said they ought to be able to come to life. Maybe he could use that same focus in the sigils to protect them.

"Yeah. Good. That's four. Let me spend some time with them and see if I can make them work," Evan said, leaning back and stretching. He saw a glint of lust in Seth's eyes and intentionally twisted, making his t-shirt ride up and expose a strip of skin above his waistband. He got up and walked over to where Seth was sitting, straddling him before sinking down onto his lap.

"I think studying makes me horny," he said with his best seductive smile. "And all this talk about magic…maybe you could polish my wand." He ground his crotch against Seth's and got a sinful groan in response.

"I can't believe you actually said that," Seth said, but Evan knew that moan hadn't been on account of a cheesy pun. Just to make sure, he rocked back and forth and felt Seth's cock grow hard against him.

Evan reached down between them, making short work of his belt and Seth's button-fly. He shoved down his own jeans as Seth wriggled loose of his constricting denim. Evan smiled when he saw that Seth was commando, and freed his own swollen prick from his boxer briefs. Seth's larger hand closed around both their cocks, working them hard and fast. He stole a kiss, open-mouthed and desperate as the sensation drove them both toward a quick-and-dirty climax.

"So close," Evan put one hand on Seth's shoulders and slid the other under his lover's shirt. He pinched a nipple, rolling the hard bud between his fingers and Seth's breath caught. "Wanna come with you."

Seconds later, Evan felt his climax flare through him. A heartbeat later, Seth's body tensed, and he shouted Evan's name as their mixed spend coated his fist. It took a few moments before Evan could manage words. He dropped forward, resting his head against Seth's neck. They stayed like that until the urgency of wiping away cooling jizz led to trying to untangle themselves without tripping over their own jeans.

"Nice study break," Seth said. "I'm 'up' for tutoring you, anytime."

Evan soaked a paper towel, rinsed it out, and lobbed it underhand at Seth's head. "Enough with the puns, already!"

Seth was still chuckling as he wiped them up and buttoned his jeans. "Hey, I've heard that positive reinforcement helps memory. So…"

"If we 'reinforce' any more, we're never going to get the job done," Evan returned, rolling his eyes.

"Speaking of which…while we're here, I saw something about people having gone missing at a local haunted house attraction over Halloween. Want to see if they got more spooks than they bargained for?"

"Where are we, anyhow?" Evan tucked away and zipped up. He looked out the trailer's window but saw nothing but a bleak mid-November landscape. Evan had been asleep in the front seat of the truck when they had arrived at their destination, rousing only when Seth woke him to come inside.

"Breezewood," Seth said, chucking the paper towel and washing his hands. "Crossroads of Pennsylvania." The Turnpike converged here with several major interstates, and the town's main industry seemed to be hotels, gas stations, convenience stores, and restaurants for weary travelers.

Evan closed up the notebooks and study materials and set up his laptop. Several *pings* told him he had new email. "So you found an article? Maybe it's a publicity stunt."

Seth shrugged. "Maybe. But if so, someone's stringing the Breezewood police along, which can't end well for the jokers."

A quick search led Evan to the article, which he pulled up on his screen. A headline read,

"*Teens Still Missing After Halloween Outing. The Breezewood Boosters' annual Scare-For-Care benefit haunted house remains under investigation after two teenagers were reported missing Halloween night. Ashley Bennett and Rod Wilson, both seventeen, were last seen going into the haunted attraction. Cameras inside the house show them reaching the halfway mark, but no one reported seeing the couple leave, and they have been reported missing by their parents. An investigation is ongoing. If anyone has information...*"

Evan sat back, frowning at the screen. "Seriously? I'm betting they conned a friend into screwing with the cameras, snuck out a side door, and ran off to West Virginia to elope."

"It's been nearly two weeks," Seth said. "If they'd just gotten hitched, don't you think they'd have told someone—or posted on social media?"

Evan rubbed a hand over his mouth. "Not if their parents were hateful about it," he said. "You were lucky to have good ones, but some of the rest of us..." He let his voice trail off.

"Point taken," Seth replied. "But hey, the idea was to start out with some easy hunts to get you warmed up." He ignored Evan's raised eyebrow, suggesting they'd already gotten plenty "warm" with earlier activities. "We're not trying to hunt down Bigfoot or the Loch Ness Monster."

"Those are real?" Evan gave a startled yelp.

Seth chuckled. "Not as far as I know, but hey, like they used to say on TV, 'the truth is out there.'"

Evan shrugged. "Okay. And if we turn up evidence that it's not supernatural, then we can let the cops do their thing."

Seth poured a cup of coffee and brought it to Evan, then went back to fix one for himself. The email pinged again. "Sounds like your inbox is busy."

Evan opened his mailbox. "Mostly coupons from places I shopped in Richmond—guess I can unsubscribe from those now," he said. He frowned as a name caught his eye. "Huh.

Got something from Liam—he was my manager at Treddy's."

He skimmed the email. Liam gave him an update on the restoration efforts after the fire that had gutted the old bar. Evan felt a stab of guilt knowing that Valac had torched Treddy's to draw him out. It didn't really make Evan responsible for the fire, but he couldn't help feeling that way. One of his old co-workers was implicated in a sensational series of murders that was making headlines—Evan winced since he'd been the intended victim. He finished and looked up to find Seth watching him with a hard-to-read expression.

"Something up?" Seth's voice sounded a little off.

"Just work gossip," Evan said, trying not to show how much his misplaced guilt bothered him. "Repairs are coming along, investigators have finally gone away, and Liam's dating someone. Izzy got a new job—not surprising since Treddy's isn't open right now—so pretty much everyone I knew is doing something else now." He wasn't really sad to leave; he knew tending bar was a port in the storm and that he'd eventually move on. But Liam and Izzy and some of the other staff had been fun to work with, and they'd taken him in when he needed it. Of course, he mused, Jackie had also tried to kill him, so it wasn't all roses.

"Evan?" Seth's tone roused him from his thoughts.

"Sorry. Nothing important, just chit-chat."

"Do you miss them?"

"Sure," Evan responded, then sighed. "I mean, I didn't really have anyone else when I moved to Richmond, and a lot of the folks at Treddy's were from out of town, so we hung out. But...we wouldn't have stayed friends if we didn't all work together. Nothing really in common." He saw uncertainty in Seth's eyes. "And no one I cared about."

Seth's lips twitched in a hint of a smile, but the questions didn't entirely fade from his eyes. Evan wondered again about the past lovers who had hurt him, and what it would take to fully win his trust. "Good to hear," Seth said in a low voice that sent heat to Evan's groin.

"So, how do we check out this haunted house?" Evan asked. He wasn't completely comfortable with the idea of going looking for danger, but then again, that was what he signed up for, joining Seth's quest, wasn't it? *I just need to be able to prove myself,* Evan thought. *Show him that I'm not going to be a liability to be left at home. So I've got to get up to speed, and fast.*

"If it's still on the news, then people are probably talking about it," Seth said. "Thought we might go hit a local joint for dinner and then find a non-tourist bar, see what we hear. Then we can drive by and get a feel for the place. Do a little recon, and go back late at night."

"You think we'll know what's behind the disappearances that fast?" Evan asked.

Seth shrugged. "If not, we'll stay another day. But it's not healthy to stick around too long. Getting noticed doesn't usually end well." Seth grabbed his laptop and sat down across from Evan. "With both of us digging, we might have a pretty good idea of what we're up against before we even go for dinner."

"Got a plan?"

"How about if you search the missing kids' social media, see what the newspapers are saying, what you can find about the victims and the haunted house attraction. I'll hack into the police files and see what the cops have turned up. And I can see if any other hunters have reported odd doings around here in the past. We won't know what we'll discover until we find it," Seth answered.

They passed the afternoon in companionable silence. Evan finished answering his few emails, happy that his new website had garnered some inquiries about graphic design services. He'd given up doing much on social media to evade his stalker ex-boyfriend, but he did keep a Facebook account that was locked down pretty tight. A quick check told him no one had posted any exciting news. *I'd lay bets that my life at the moment is way more "exciting" than any of my friends. If by "exciting" you mean running from monsters and the cops, and hunting immortal psycho warlocks.* If he had guarded his privacy jealously before, he was likely to be even more careful about what he said online from now on.

Once those tasks were out of the way, Evan dug into the case. Ashley's accounts showed a lot of selfies with her legion of best friends, pictures of her cheerleading squad, and shots of her with her dog. One or two of the photos featured her in a clinch with a nerdy-in-a-cute-way dark-haired boy Evan guessed to be Rod. Nothing in any of the posts suggested they were serious enough to run off to Vegas and get hitched.

Rod's posts were fewer, mostly pictures of him with the basketball team, and a couple with Ashley. Evan wondered if they hadn't been dating long; there weren't enough photos to suggest much of a history. *Interesting. So much for the easy theory.*

The news articles all looked like they came from the same police statement. Beyond stating the basic facts, and making an appeal for information, the articles just rehashed what they'd said before.

Now that's interesting, Evan thought as he followed a link that led him to a blog instead of a news site. "So, get this," he said, making Seth look up from his screen.

"There's a guy who blogs as…The Thin Man. Runs a paranormal site that looks local. The design sucks."

"And?" Seth asked, probably suspecting Evan hadn't interrupted him for a critique of the website's layout.

"Sorry. He posted a couple of days ago about the disappearances. Claims that the building they're using for the attraction is has a history that includes a deadly lover's quarrel, a fatal burglary, at least one suicide, a few dodgy disappearances, and several at-home deaths blamed on everything from cholera, back in the day, to the flu," Evan said. The writing was amateurish and sensational, with a disturbing lack of noted sources, but the author's prose gushed with passion for his topic.

"Has the guy posted anything else?" Seth asked in a tone that suggested he was open to taking the information seriously.

Evan scrolled down. "There's something about ghosts in an old turnpike tunnel that isn't used anymore, and instructions on where to go to see a ghostly car wreck that repeats on rainy fall nights."

Seth nodded. "Sounds about right. There's a database that Milo uses—and I think Mark's researcher friend, Chiara, too. They all contribute information about supernatural activity that doesn't require a hunt. I had a look while you were sleeping. The tunnel and the ghostly car wreck are both on the local list. The activity might be real and definitely supernatural, but it's not harmful. Which doesn't prove that the guy knows what he's talking about for everything, but he's not wrong on those."

Evan checked the time. "It's still early. Let me see if I can find anything else. Having any luck?"

Seth shook his head. "The cops really don't know much. They've talked to both families and a lot of the kids' friends. Running off would be out of character. Good grades, no problems at school, no prior trouble with the law, no evidence of drugs. No long-standing grudges, vengeful exes or jealous, mean girls. The cops went over the haunted house and tore all the displays apart, looked for hidden doors, walled-over closets—nothing. They're considering bringing in a psychic."

Evan raised his eyebrows at that. "Think it'll work?"

"Maybe. I asked my folklore guy, Simon Kincaide, about it. He's that psychic medium in Myrtle Beach I told you about. Just helped catch a serial killer. He said it depends on whether the cops find a real psychic or not."

"So, do we get involved?"

Seth leaned back. "A psychic isn't going to tell the cops if there's a supernatural creature involved. They wouldn't believe it, anyhow. If we check into it and don't find anything, then we move on and let them handle it. But if this *is* some kind of creature, then the cops either won't figure it out, or they won't know how to take care of the problem."

Evan finished off his now-cold coffee. "All right. I've got some ideas I want to chase. Do you think any of your official sources could confirm anything in the Thin Man's article?"

"I can look—although names and dates would be nice," Seth snarked.

Chasing down information online was like a game, and Evan found himself caught up in the puzzle. Seth came up with the names of the house's previous owners, and Evan dug through online records, old digitized newspapers, and obituaries to track down details. An hour later, his rumbling stomach demanded that he set the search aside.

"People didn't come straight out and say things like 'murder' and 'suicide,' but from what they *didn't* say, or the *way* they said things, I think that at least some of the rumors are true," Evan reported.

"That's what I'd pick up from the way the property got transferred," Seth said. "Boring stuff, public records, unless you know how to make them cough up the juicy dirt. From what I could find, the house sat empty for a while between the last residents and when it got bought to make the attraction. There's a pretty lengthy list of police reports about strange lights, people seeing shadowy figures around the house, that kind of thing. Nothing ever came of it, and the cops seem to think it was all urban legend stuff—people saw things because they heard stories about the house."

"Maybe," Evan allowed, drumming his fingers as he thought. "I went through the photos people had posted of the attraction's rooms decked out in all their glory. I thought maybe they might have gotten something like the Ellison painting—something that really *was* haunted." He shook his head. "Everything I saw looked pretty hokey, like the stuff they sell in those Halloween shops."

Seth looked up. "I hear an unspoken 'but' coming…"

Evan nodded. "I looked for missing persons reports from the area. Every year, a couple of people go missing while the haunted house is running. Not necessarily missing from the house or that they were reported anywhere near it, but during the period it's open. The other reports seemed randomly distributed throughout the year. But there was a spike, every time, in October."

"I'll take a look in the police files and see what comes up," Seth agreed. Evan wondered if he should have been more concerned over Seth's hacking, and decided he could go along with bending a few laws for a good cause.

"You're right," Seth said after several minutes. "No bodies ever found, no connection to the haunted house—no one even speculating they're related until this last pair of disappearances—but there's a correlation, all right. And I bet it means something." Seth closed his laptop. "Let's get dinner, and then head to a bar. Nothing else to do—not like there was anything on TV," he added with a smirk.

Evan climbed onto the back of the Hayabusa. Last night they hadn't worn helmets, because there'd have been no way to get the ghoul guts out of the padding. Tonight, they both suited up, unwilling to get taken out by a pothole after they survived fighting monsters.

Supper at the Roost Diner passed uneventfully. Seth and Evan ate without much conversation, trying to listen in on the discussions around them. No one seemed inclined to discuss the "murder house" or the disappearances, and the local news channel on the TV in one corner only ran a quick announcement that the investigation was "ongoing," with a crawl of the police tip line at the bottom of the screen.

Fortunately, the food was good. Evan dug into a helping of homemade fried chicken with mashed potatoes he couldn't possibly finish, although Seth managed to polish off all of his hamburger steak with gravy. The coffee lived up to the best diner expectations. Seth let out a satisfied burp as they returned to the motorcycle, and gave an only slightly apologetic grin as Evan muttered something about "frat boys."

"Hey, a good meal is a thing of beauty," Seth said with a shrug. "Let's see what we find out at the bar."

"Maybe it's just not a hot topic anymore," Evan said as they reached for their helmets. "Except, of course, for the families of the kids who went missing. People have short memories unless there's another incident."

Seth frowned. "That's just it though. There've been disappearances every year around this time. Surely someone noticed?"

Evan shrugged. "Maybe not, if the missing people weren't always connected to the haunted house. And people go missing for lots of reasons—runaways, bad debts, relationships gone wrong. This seems like a pretty transient place."

"Maybe. One way or the other, we'll figure it out." Evan snugged up against Seth on the bike as they headed for the bar. He leaned in, wrapping his arms tight, bracketing Seth's hips with his, thigh to thigh with the vibration of the bike beneath them. The contact and the movement were far more of a turn-on than Evan ever imagined, and the little thrill of fear he still felt from being on a motorcycle heightened all his senses. As usual, he had to adjust himself when they reached the parking lot and smirked when Seth shifted a bit as well when he dismounted.

"Told you there'd be something to like about the bike," Seth said with a knowing smile.

"Oh, there is. Definitely."

The Plucked Duck bar and grill didn't look like it attracted many tourists. Other than a few big rigs parked off to one side, the lot was full of pickup trucks and a few other motor-cycles, all with Pennsylvania plates. By agreement, Seth and Evan entered separately, in part to be able to split up and hopefully overhear more gossip, and also because they didn't feel like testing the social tolerances of the local wildlife. Evan found a seat at the bar, while Seth wandered over to a table where he could sit with his back to the wall, able to watch both the door and Evan.

"What'll it be?"

Evan looked up at the bartender's question. He had expected someone older, maybe even his father's age, to be tending bar in a place like the Duck. A handsome thirty-something with frosted blond spikes and a pierced eyebrow surprised him.

"Got Yuengling?" Evan replied, not wanting to sound like a beer snob, but unwilling to down a Michelob, even to solve the murders.

The bartender grinned. "Finally! Someone with taste." He popped open a bottle and set it in front of Evan, letting his finger trace down through the condensation as he intention-ally met Evan's gaze. "Wanna give me your card so I can start a tab?"

Evan returned his smile. "No tab. Just cash." He pulled out some bills—including a nice tip—and set them on the table.

"Just passing through? I don't remember you." His tone suggested that he definitely would have recalled seeing Evan before. The bartender's name tag said "*Ricky*." Given his own experiences, Evan figured it was fake.

"Yeah. Aren't most people?" He took a drink, tipping the bottle as he tilted his head back, exposing his throat. He noticed the bartender noticing.

Ricky leaned against the backbar. "Breezewood is that kind of place," he said with a shrug. "Me, I'm a native."

Oh, really? Evan thought. "Then you've heard about that

whole haunted house thing that's on the news? Kinda weird, isn't it?"

Ricky hesitated, as if he really wouldn't have picked that topic for conversation, then Evan noticed his gaze fall to the way Evan's fingers stroked the beer bottle. Before he could answer, a middle-aged man in a gimme cap at the other end of the bar hailed him for another Bud. Ricky poured a pint from the tap and gave it to the thirsty trucker, then checked on three men farther down the counter, before returning, just a little too attentively, to where Evan sat.

"Breezewood is a weird kind of place, you know?" Ricky said, segueing back into the conversation. "People come and go all the time. Especially in the fall. Maybe they can't stand the thought of another PA winter. Takes a special kind." He regarded Evan. "You're not from around here, are you?"

Evan smiled. "Nope. Virginia."

"Thought I heard an accent. I like the South. Finger-lickin' good, you know?" His smile made his intent clear, if Evan had any doubt.

"So you think the kids at the haunted house just skipped town?" Evan asked, trying not to sound too interested.

Then again, from the signals Ricky was sending, he'd probably be happy to discuss the weather, complete with innuendo. Evan didn't think much about Ricky's flirting. When he'd tended bar at Treddy's, being whatever the customers wanted him to be—within reason—paid off in tips. If Ricky's gaydar had picked up on Evan that fast, maybe the guy didn't get many opportunities to bat his eyes at someone. *It's not like I'm going to do anything about it. And we might get some information.*

Ricky looked from one side to another. At first, Evan thought he might just be checking to see if any of the barflies needed a refresh. Then Ricky leaned over confidentially, so only Evan heard his next words. "There's something wrong about that house. One of my friends went in there on a dare when we were kids, and we never saw him again. People said he ran away, but Joey wouldn't have done that. After that, we always said the wicked witch lived there." He shook his head. "And then they made it into one of those stupid haunted houses? You couldn't pay me to go in that place."

Ricky straightened when one of the men called for another shot. Evan sipped his beer, then chanced a look over his shoulder toward where he'd seen Seth sitting. He wasn't prepared for the look in Seth's eyes, a mixture of hurt, anger, and possessiveness that raised a tangle of feelings in his belly.

Shit. Seth had seen his exchange with Ricky and was taking it way too seriously. Was he remembering their flirty beginning, and wondering if Evan made it a habit? His heart sank. If he had watched Seth do the same to chat up a witness, Evan could imagine how it would have felt. This thing between them was intense but too new, too fragile.

They had been running for their lives and fallen into each other's arms. But sooner or later, for their relationship to work, Evan knew they had to do the hard work of actually getting to know each other beyond the great sex, and that scared him. His first boyfriend had betrayed him to their church and community, getting Evan thrown out of his home. His second real relationship ended in violence and a restraining order.

I'm not good at this stuff. What if I've screwed it all up? He tamped his insecurities down, and at the same time, a niggle of anger flared. *Or did I pick wrong again? I thought Mike was sexy because he had an edge of danger—until it got used against me. He got mean when he was jealous, controlling. Shit. What if Seth's the same way? It's not like we really know each other.*

Ricky came back after he'd served the other customers and cashed out several tabs. "So, if you're in town tonight," he began.

"I can't," Evan blurted. "I'm seeing someone."

Ricky gave a pointed glance to the empty barstools on

either side of Evan. "I don't *see* anyone. Like they say, if you can't be with the one you love…"

Evan felt the beer sour in his stomach. He wanted to go to Seth and explain, even while part of him rebelled that he should be able to talk to anyone he wanted to, that he hadn't done anything wrong and shouldn't feel guilty. Suddenly, Evan needed to get out of there, feeling claustrophobic even through the Duck was hardly packed to capacity.

"Hey man, you got any smokes?" Evan asked. Ricky pulled out his own pack and shook one loose for him.

"On the house," he said with a sly smile, producing a lighter from his pocket and handing it to Evan. "Gotta take it outside though. Bring the lighter back, or I'll have to pat you down for it," he added with a wink.

Fuck, that just made the whole mess worse. Evan mumbled his thanks, grabbed the cigarette and lighter, and made for the door. He bumped into someone on the way and barely muttered an apology in his haste. Outside, he stepped to the side of the doorway, still remaining in the bright glare of the security bulbs. His hand shook as he lit up, and he took a long drag, closing his eyes and hoping it would calm his nerves.

"I didn't know you smoked." Seth's voice at his elbow made Evan drop the lighter when he startled.

"I don't, much," Evan said, afraid to look at Seth, fearful of what he might see in his eyes. "Just when I'm really nervous."

"Looked like you made a friend." Seth's voice was carefully neutral. When Evan turned to face him, he couldn't read anything in his gaze, as if Seth had shuttered his expression.

Is he angry? Jealous? Does he care—or not? Shit, we never discussed being exclusive, with the whole running for our lives stuff, and then suddenly living together. Maybe he wants an open relationship. Maybe he doesn't do commitment.

And if that was the case, then they were doomed. Evan didn't have a lot of experience, but he did know from the hook-ups he'd had that he wasn't cut out for casual sex. He wanted a forever man, the kind of lifelong commitment he'd seen with his parents and grandparents, only with a guy.

And yet. Seth looked tense, like he was ready for a fight. Was he going to unleash his anger on Evan? Or didn't he care enough to be bothered? Neither alternative was good.

Fear and worry curdled into anger, and Evan faced Seth defiantly. "Nothing happened," he snapped. "Just a little friendly conversation—and I got some intel." He turned his head and puffed out smoke. It had been a long time since he'd had a cigarette—he was never much of a smoker, and he'd quit a while ago—and now he hated the taste in his mouth and the burn in his throat.

"Well, we came here to be friendly," Seth replied, his eyes darkening. The tight set to his jaw made his anger clear.

"Look, do you want to know what I found out or not?" Evan could be a stubborn bastard, too. He flicked the cig away, ground it out on the gravel, picked up the dropped lighter and then drew himself up to his full height, almost daring Seth to take a swing and, simultaneously, fearing that he would.

Seth went completely, eerily still, giving away nothing in his expression. "Yeah. So what did you get?"

Evan related the conversation about the disappearances, doing his best to make it clinical and devoid of any hint of flirting. Seth listened, frowning as Evan wrapped up his tale.

"Sounds like a *Muma Pădurii,*" Seth replied. "Romanian folklore. Probably where the Hansel and Gretel stories came from. Down South, they call it a Boo Hag. Lures people in, then eats them."

"You still want to go after it?" They needed to talk, to sort out this tension between them, to get down to answers—good or bad. But they had come to do a job, and stop the killing. Right now, that was more important, Evan told himself. And despite how pissed he was at Seth for reading too much into

61

his conversation with Ricky, for not having faith in him to stay true, Evan didn't want to rush that dreaded conversation, in case the knowing was worse than the uncertainty.

"Yeah. They aren't too hard to banish once you know what you're fighting. We've got everything we need." Seth's voice sounded cold, professional. Maybe he'd just gone to the soldier inside to be clear-headed for the battle yet to come. Maybe. But it felt to Evan like Seth had pulled back, and coldness settled on him that had nothing to do with the autumn chill in the air.

"So...are we done here?" Evan asked.

"Yeah, for tonight."

"I'll be right back." Evan stepped back into the bar and set the lighter on the counter. Ricky was at the other end of the bar but caught Evan's eye with a questioning look. Evan smiled and waved but didn't stick around.

Seth was stiff and practically glaring when Evan returned. He turned, climbed on the bike, and started it without saying a word.

Evan swung up behind Seth on the Hayabusa, and slipped his arms around his lover's waist. He thought he felt Seth tense up, draw away just a bit instead of leaning back or pulling Evan forward to be plastered together like on the ride there. Evan's mind whirled as they drove through the darkness.

How did things go so wrong so fast, and can I fix them? I don't like being mistrusted, but I guess I wouldn't have liked seeing Seth flirt with someone, either. Shit. I've made a mess of things, and if he didn't already wonder if I could handle myself, now who knows what he thinks about how I feel about him? Does he want a forever-something or just a good-for-now? We said we loved each other, in the heat of the moment. But does he mean it the way I mean it? Or was it just the adrenaline talking?

When they got back to the RV, Seth was all business. He rummaged through the storage beneath the trailer, opening the secret compartment where he kept the special weapons and equipment that would be impossible to explain if they ever got searched at a traffic stop.

"It's a witch-vampire," Seth called over his shoulder as Evan waited, holding his helmet. "It can steal its victim's breath and life energy, or take the person's skin and 'ride' them until the body falls apart. My bet is that something drew the hag to the house, and it attached itself to the place."

"How do we fight it?" Evan asked, wracking his brain for what he had read in the lore about witches. There was so much to learn, and he didn't trust the things he'd seen on TV shows.

Seth loaded the duffel bag with salt, iron weapons, throwing knives, their sawed-off shotguns, and other objects Evan couldn't quickly identify. "Salt and iron can cut their power. Mistletoe, hazel, hemlock, and garlic make it harder for them to trap you with their magic."

He held out a small burlap bag stitched closed at the top. "It's kind of like a gris-gris bag," Seth said. "Has a little of all those things in it, plus I had a priest bless it. Keep it on you," he added as Evan took the bag and pocketed it, and Seth slipped one into his own jacket. "It's not bulletproof, but it can make you slippery to their magic." Seth also grabbed a squirt bottle of holy water, which went into the pack.

Finally, Seth held up a sturdy glass globe with a long neck. "Witch bottle," he said, displaying it for Evan. "If we can find something tangible that belongs to the witch, we can trap her in here. Throw it on the fire, and the witch goes 'poof.'"

"Where do you think we'll find her?" Evan asked. "Maybe we should wait until tomorrow and scout the place in daylight."

"In a hurry to go back to the Duck?" Seth sounded like he was looking for a fight.

"Not really. Unless you fancy a threesome," Evan shot back. He was almost too annoyed to notice the flash of hurt in

Seth's eyes. Almost, but not quite, and to see the way Seth's cheeks had gone pink.

Shit, we've got to stop sniping at each other. This isn't helping. And he doesn't know that I'd never do that. I'm not the sharing kind. Evan immediately regretted his comment, and he wondered if Seth felt bad about his dig, also. But when Seth didn't apologize, Evan choked down his own apology and turned away.

"Not my thing," Seth said, but his voice was flat. "Anyhow. We go over, try to draw out the witch, and trap her. Come back, and drive away." He paused like he thought about saying something else, then didn't, and hefted the bag.

"We should take the truck."

Evan looked up, surprised. He tried to figure out what had changed Seth's mind. "The bike's easier to hide."

"They catch us with the duffel bag, we're screwed."

"Then we'd better not get caught." Evan wasn't quite sure how they had dug in on opposite sides, with him arguing for the bike. Did Seth not trust him on the back? Evan had been proud of how much he had gotten over his initial reluctance. He'd almost been verging on enjoying the ride, under better circumstances. Or did Seth not want him so close, clinging to him? *Fuck. All of a sudden, everything's gone wrong. And I don't know how to fix it.*

Maybe if they finished off the witch and came back high on the success of a good hunt, it would be easier to talk to Seth, assure him that Evan had no interested in Ricky—or anyone else, and talk through what had prompted Seth's jealousy.

Maybe he had a boyfriend who cheated on him. That could explain the reaction. But another, darker possibility rose in his mind. *What if he didn't intend to be exclusive, or he doesn't want a commitment even though we're living together?* That sat in Evan's gut like a rock. He'd fallen hard for Seth, and while they'd ended up on the road—and on the run—out of necessity, it had all felt so right. *We have to get it out in the open sometime. And if what he wants isn't what I want...I guess he can drop me off in Pittsburgh.* Evan didn't linger on the thought. He knew he'd be devastated if that happened, and it didn't bear dwelling on when they had a job to do.

"Hey, you with me?" Seth asked, the sharp edge to his voice rousing Evan from his thoughts.

"Yeah. Yeah. Let's get done, and get gone," Evan agreed. He slung the heavy pack across his back, shoulder to opposite hip to balance its weight, then he walked over to the black bike and pulled his helmet on, waiting for Seth to catch up.

Seth gave him a look as if he were trying to decipher Evan's thoughts, then muttered something under his breath and swung onto the bike, sending up a spray of dirt behind them as they peeled out of the campground.

THE BREEZEWOOD HORROR HOUSE LOOKED THE PART, WITH trails of yellow police tape flapping in the breeze and the dim, flickering security light. *All they needed was ominous movie music,* Evan thought as he climbed off the bike and waited while Seth walked it into the shadows. They paused in a dark spot to pull a few weapons from the bag before Seth zipped it back up and hefted it himself, not offering an explanation. Evan couldn't help feeling like he'd been somehow demoted.

He remembered the fear in Ricky's voice when the bartender had mentioned the childhood friend gone missing. That hadn't been contrived, and it certainly wasn't part of a pick-up line. Ricky had been genuinely scared. Evan thought about the pattern of disappearances and wondered what unholy bargain bound the house and the witch together. Given how long people had been vanishing, whoever angered the witch or made a deal with her was probably long dead, well beyond mortal ability to punish. That mattered less than stopping the cycle and freeing Breezewood from its grim annual harvest.

They looked up at the "haunted" old house from the front. The peeling paint and splintered casements suggested that without serious renovation, the historic home would not survive many more seasons. "Cops tore the inside apart looking for the missing teens," Seth said, all business. "And you've seen the promo shots of the interior—it's movie props and high school drama department-level staging. No real antiques, no family heirlooms."

"So nothing that was likely to anchor a witch," Evan supplied.

Seth gave a curt nod, grudging approval. "Yeah. So there's got to be something else. Let's have a look around."

They circled the wood frame house and spotted a small, overgrown stone building toward the back edge of the property. "What's that?" Evan asked.

"Looks like a spring house," Seth replied, training his green-filtered flashlight on the crumbling masonry. The small stone shed was built of stacked stone with a shingle roof, about the size of a large closet. It looked older than the main house, and Evan remembered that wooden homes often burned and were rebuilt. He eyed the structure, wondering what secrets it held. They both selected weapons from the cache and stood back to survey the territory.

"I'm going to lay down a salt circle, and you can cover me," Seth said. "I'll be bait."

Evan shook his head. "Fuck that. You shoot, I'll draw it out."

"I am not using you for bait."

Something in the tone of Seth's pronouncement raised Evan's hackles.

"Because you don't think I can handle it?"

"This is not the time."

"Then lay down the goddamn circle and let me do what I can do!"

She was on them before Seth had finished the salt circle. *Muma Pădurii*, Boo Hag, or Old Nonna, the witch-ghost swept down onto them like the wrath of God, shrieking with a voice like steel against slate and clawing at them with her sharp nails.

The hag hit Evan first, knocking him away from the protective circle, sending him staggering and then tackling him to the ground with unexpected strength. She pinned him to the wet earth with her bony knees and sinewy muscle, pressing down on his chest with a weight that did not match her scrawny, ghastly appearance.

Suddenly, Evan found it difficult to breathe. He struggled to pull air into his chest, and when he exhaled, he saw the vapor that left his mouth emit a faint, white glow as if it carried with it some of his soul, his essence. He remembered what Seth had said about the Boo Hag, how it sucked the life from its victims, and he bucked and twisted to get free, even as it weakened him with every breath.

Evan saw a rush of movement and saw a swift downward motion as something stabbed the hag in the back. She screamed, and her whole body stiffened and arched. He took the chance to break free, throwing her off and scrabbling away. The hag turned her malice on Seth, who had driven a hawthorn stake through her ribs, and she moved faster than expected, grabbing his shoulder with her pointed, razor-sharp nails and digging in. Blood colored his shirt where she impaled him on her claws, and she opened her black-lipped mouth, as her red eyes glowed with hunger, and then she inhaled, drawing Seth's life from him.

Evan saw his chance and lunged. He thrust an iron knife into the Boo Hag's scrawny neck, sharp edge turned toward her spine, with his right hand. With his left, he rammed a thin, sharpened skewer of mistletoe between her ribs where her heart should have been. She let go of Seth, and her too-long arms clawed at the air behind her, as Evan used the saw-bladed knife to hack through her spine and send the head rolling.

Seth dropped to his hands and knees, weakened by the Boo Hag's attack. Evan felt the effects as well, but he was still coursing with adrenaline from seeing Seth in her clutches. He stuffed his gris-gris bag in the dead witch's mouth, cut off a hank of hair and tucked it into the witch bottle, and pulled containers of salt and purifying herbs from the duffel, liberally sprinkling them over the hag's body. Evan wasn't sure what to expect, whether the corpse would catch on fire or shrivel to a husk, but when it and the severed head vanished altogether, he stood staring at the empty ground, slack-jawed with astonishment. Then he kicked dry leaves into the old stone spring house, set the witch bottle atop them, and tossed in a match to set the pile alight.

Seth staggered to his feet and came toward him. Evan braced for an argument, maybe even a punch. Instead, Seth pulled him close, wrapping his arms tightly around him, locking him in an embrace.

"I'm sorry," Seth said, over and over, his cheek pressed against the top of Evan's head. "I got so angry, thought you had changed your mind about me...us...and then she went after you, and you could have died, and...I didn't care about anything except getting her off you."

Evan wrapped his arms around Seth's waist and squeezed tight, aware of the warm, sticky flow of blood where the crone's claws had pierced Seth's shoulder. "I had to stop her from hurting you," he replied, breathing in the scent of Seth's sweat and letting it calm him. "But you're bleeding, and we need to get out of here. So we can talk—"

"We need to talk—"

"Can you drive?" Evan asked, knowing that they had to leave before anyone noticed the smoke.

"Yeah. I think so," Seth said, though his voice sounded shaky to Evan. They gathered the weapons and supplies that had scattered from the bag and headed for the Hayabusa. Evan ripped Seth's bloody sleeve to make a temporary bandage, staunching the blood flow until they could get back to the trailer. He wasn't fooled into thinking the injury was minor; he could see the way Seth favored his arm, but he also knew he wasn't yet ready to drive the motorcycle. Evan climbed on behind, snuggling up against Seth this time and feeling Seth lean back just a little against him, validating. Then they headed out, with Evan's arms tight around Seth's waist, and roared into the night.

4

SETH

I'M SORRY. I'M SO FUCKIN' SORRY. SETH WORKED OUT HIS confession as he lay awake that night, listening to Evan breathing, deep in sleep. To Seth's relief, Evan hadn't insisted on taking the couch, although he would have been within his rights after Seth had been such an asshole at the bar. Seth's arm throbbed, despite the ibuprofen he'd swallowed. Evan had insisted on cleaning and treating his wound, and Seth had finally stopped protesting, feeling even more ashamed of himself at Evan's gentle touch.

When is he going to figure out what I already know? He could do so much better. Evan's just getting a taste of what staying with me really means. Living on the road, avoiding the cops. Getting hurt. Nearly getting killed. Why would a guy like him put up with that when he could have a normal life?

Seth had replaced Evan's electronics because it was the right thing to do after the fire cost him everything. But to Seth, it was also giving Evan his freedom, his ticket out. Sure, Evan was welcome to stay for as long as he needed to get his business off the ground and some money in the bank. Seth would grieve the day Evan left, but he wouldn't begrudge him the chance to get his life back on track. Seth couldn't help bracing for that day to come.

And that's why I made such an ass of myself at the bar, Seth thought, wincing as he recalled his anger and jealousy. He didn't think Evan intended to cheat on him; Evan wasn't the type. But seeing that hot bartender hitting on Evan just served to remind Seth how easy it would be for Evan to move on after they parted.

He'll find someone new. And I'll be alone again. Seth blinked as his eyes stung at the thought, and he let his hand slip over so that his fingers brushed against Evan's arm. They had been too drained by the fight against the hag—and Seth's arm had throbbed too much—for them to consider fucking away the tension, and they had fallen asleep before they could have the conversation Seth dreaded.

They'd both been off their game last night, with the argument brewing between them. Seth had been stupid and bullheaded to let them hunt like that, putting them both in danger. And Evan had done so well. He'd willingly gone along with the training regimen Seth had set for them, running and sparring in the early morning, free weights and boxing, shooting and knife skills. He had been game for learning rote magic, something that was difficult and dangerous, in order to keep up. Then they'd gone in half-cocked because of Seth's stupid ego and nearly gotten themselves killed.

Evan had saved his life. Again. And they'd both come home wounded. Now, Seth wondered how he could properly apologize, and whether it was even possible to fix the hurt feelings between them.

I love him, but I suck at relationships. Not like I've ever had a real one, a good one. I don't regret falling for Evan, but guys like me don't get to keep guys like him. I've got nothing to offer except pain, fear, and an early grave. He deserves better. Seth knew that in between all the research for their latest hunts, Evan had thrown himself into getting his fledgling business off the ground, and he'd already had inquiries from prospective new clients. Between what Seth had seen of Evan's talent for graphic design and the photography he'd shot in their rare free moments, Seth didn't doubt that the business would be a success, and soon.

Maybe he's just biding his time, preparing his exit strategy. And we're making a memory, something to look back on when it's over. Seth hoped with all his heart that he was wrong, but deep inside, he couldn't imagine why Evan would choose to stay.

The quiet hum of Seth's phone vibrating on the nightstand rescued him from his thoughts. Evan snuffled and rolled over, and Seth indulged himself with a lingering, fond look before he grabbed the phone and eased himself out of bed, careful not to wake his partner. He grabbed his robe and pushed his feet into sheepskin moccasins since the RV had cooled down overnight.

Seth padded into the kitchen and answered the call as he got the coffee maker going. "Hey, Mark. What's up?" he greeted his friend and fellow monster hunter, Mark Wojcik.

"Where are you guys?" Mark asked, sounding like he'd been up all night.

"Ligonier. I put some miles behind us and the Boo Hag house in Breezewood last night. Why?"

"Everything go all right?"

Seth sighed. "As good as it ever does. No one was maimed, no one died."

"I hear you," Mark agreed. "You want another 'easy' job? Got one in your backyard, so to speak."

Did he want another job? If Evan intended to stay, whether for a while or forever, he needed the experience. And if this life wasn't right for him, Evan needed to figure that out, too. "Sure," Seth said, wondering if Mark could hear the conflicted emotions in his voice.

"Don't bowl me over with enthusiasm," Mark teased.

"You said Ligonier? There's a defunct ski resort between there and Irwin, that isn't as abandoned as it should be."

"Ghosts? Ghouls? Meth heads?"

"My source thinks zombies," Mark said. "No reports of a necromancer around there, so it could be some kid messing around with a grimoire he found online or one of those weird energy fluxes we've been getting when they frack in certain places." Fracking—a controversial way of pumping out natural gas from inside shale—caused a lot of unexpected supernatural problems by disturbing the deep places.

"And it turns out that the ski resort was built on what used to be an old family farm—complete with a private cemetery. There's a fracking operation not far from there, which is what we figure caused the problem," Mark continued.

"I hate zombies."

Mark snickered. "Think of them as cheap target practice. You shoulda seen the pack we took out at a graveyard up here in my neck of the woods. I gotta say, I'm really proud of how Sara took the whole thing in stride."

"She's hunting now?" Seth asked, surprised.

"She's a remarkable woman," Mark agreed. "She's known about hunters for a while, up in the Big Woods where she runs her B&B. But a couple of times now, I've gotten called in on something in the middle of a date, and she just rolls with it. Pretty damn impressive."

"You're a lucky man," Seth agreed, impatiently waiting for the coffee to finish brewing.

"Things going okay with you and Evan?" Mark asked as if he had a sixth sense for trouble.

Seth leaned back against the counter and scrubbed a hand over his eyes. He hadn't shaved, and the stubble was rough against his palm. "I don't know, Mark. How do you ask someone to live this kind of crazy life? Why would anyone stick around?"

Mark let out a long-suffering sigh. "If they stick around,

it's not for the life. It's because they're crazy in love—emphasis maybe on the crazy—with you. Don't try to explain it or over-think it. Just accept it as a gift."

"I screwed up, Mark. I was a real asshole last night."

"You think that comes as a surprise to anyone who knows you?" Mark teased. "And are you really asking me, of all people, for relationship advice?" He kept going before Seth could answer. "Here's what I do when I make a fool of myself. I apologize. Then I grovel. A bribe or two doesn't hurt. But mostly, I just tell her I was frickin' stupid and wrong and throw myself on her mercy. It's worked so far."

Seth could hear the grateful surprise in Mark's voice, and he knew that not too long ago, Mark had also been resigned to remaining alone after his wife left him. Maybe, Seth thought, if Mark had found someone willing to take a risk, perhaps Seth could still work things out with Evan.

"So you just want me to go over to the ski resort and play whack-a-mole?" Seth asked, shifting the conversation back to something more comfortable.

"That's what the intel says. But you know it's not usually as simple as it looks."

"That would take all the fun out if it, now wouldn't it?" Seth replied. "I'll go take a look. And Mark? Thanks."

"Try not to get your head bashed in," Mark replied, dodging more caring and sharing. "Let me know how it goes."

Seth ended the call, just as the coffee maker wheezed the last drips into the carafe. He poured a cup and snagged a muffin from the counter, thinking over the zombie job. A glance at his phone to gauge the distance made up his mind.

I'm not going to drag Evan into this, not after last night. I could go over now, let him sleep, and be back before he even notices. That way, he won't get hurt. The fact that it also avoided the looming, awkward conversation didn't escape Seth, but he chose not to think too hard on it right then.

Seth got a shower at the campground bathhouse and used the spare change of clothing he kept in the truck. He left a note for Evan in the kitchen: *"Gone to handle something, back soon. Get some rest."* Seth hesitated on how to end the note, then closed his eyes, wished for luck, and wrote, *"love, Seth."* He hoped Evan still felt the same, but Seth was resolved to hang on as long as he could see a chance.

He walked the Hayabusa a distance from the trailer to keep from waking Evan with its rumble when he pulled out. Zombies didn't require a lot of extra equipment, mostly his Glock, a machete, and a small sledgehammer, along with salt and lighter fluid. That fit in the bike's saddlebag, so Seth didn't have to worry about the duffel's weight and awkwardness, or field difficult questions should he draw the attention of the highway patrol.

He took back roads toward the now-defunct Snow Haven Ski Resort, opening up the throttle and letting the speed whisk his cares away. For a little while, at least, nothing existed except the bike and the road, and taking the curves at full speed kept him focused on the sheer joy of driving.

Seth reached the chained-shut entrance gates to the resort in less than half an hour. The archway over the ski lodge's drive looked weathered and forgotten, paint peeling and weeds rising hip-high around the posts. He might not have been able to go farther with his truck, but the bike maneuvered easily around the steel gate, and he headed up the cracked asphalt road, alert for danger.

The road took a bend, and then revealed Snow Haven's lodge. The A-frame building had a vaguely Alpine feel, with huge windows and wide balconies. *Must have been a real bitch to heat in the winter,* Seth thought. Small utility buildings— probably for skis and equipment—dotted the rolling lawn, which now looked more like a field of brown hay. Behind the lodge, near the slopes, hulked the rusting remnants of the ski lifts, with chairs still dangling from the steel cables.

Seth paused for a moment to assess the territory. He didn't intend to chase zombies around a deserted ski chalet and fall through a rotting floor to his death. If the zombies came from the farm cemetery, then they probably wouldn't head into the lodge anyhow. Without a ready supply of human victims, hungry zombies would likely prey on rabbits, squirrels, and other unlucky small creatures. The nearby woods offered a zombie smorgasbord, but Seth had brought something even better—a package of raw chicken he picked up on the way to the resort.

Seth put his phone on silent and buttoned it into an inner pocket to protect it. The Glock went into his waistband, he had a Ka-Bar in a sheath on his belt and a machete in hand, plenty of lighter fluid and holy water in small squirt bottles and a few other items in his pockets. He slung the small sledgehammer over his shoulder.

A trek up the hill to the chalet got his blood pumping. According to a text Mark sent, there was an old service roadway that ran between the ski resort and the original farm, probably for storing and hauling heavy supplies. Seth thought about moving the motorcycle, but the loud engine might scare off the zombies before he ever had a chance to put them down.

He headed back the overgrown road on foot, staying alert to every noise. The woods were quieter than usual, which set his nerves on edge. Half a dozen zombies should be no problem. But what if Mark's intel was wrong? What if the whole damn cemetery rose? Suddenly, Seth's decision to come alone no longer seemed like a good idea.

I hunted by myself before I met Evan. Most guys hunt alone their entire lives—however long that lasts. He needed time to recover from the last fight. Seth's excuses sounded hollow, even to himself. He hadn't wanted to face Evan yet and have another argument, or hash out what happened in the inevitable *conversation*. And somehow, running away to fight a pack of zombies single-handedly had seemed like a good alternative.

He stopped before he got too far down the road, an easy sprint from the open area below the chairlifts. With his Glock in his right hand, Seth shook the raw chicken out of the bag and onto the grass.

"Here, zombies," he called in a quiet falsetto. "Got some chicken for you. Tastes like long pig."

He turned and jogged back up the road, and as he went, he sprayed air freshener to mask his scent. Once he was at the edge of the clearing, easily within range of his handgun, he stopped and waited. Growls and snuffling in the trees let him know that the zombies had noticed the bait. Seth wished that salt circles worked against zombies because he would have liked to have a protective ring, but no such luck. Now, he had to watch and wait—and hope he wasn't on the menu.

Movement in the brush had Seth dropping into a firing stance. Four zombies shuffled out of the woods, still dressed in the tattered finery they'd worn in their coffins. They sniffed the air, and Seth stood absolutely still, letting out the breath he held when they turned their attention back to the plump, raw chicken.

Four shots rang out, and four zombies fell, their heads blown apart by the bullets. A growl behind him had Seth wheeling, firing on instinct rather than sight. Another zombie went down, this time a chest shot, so while he was on the ground, he wasn't out of the game. Before Seth could make the kill, two more zombies closed in from either side.

Obviously, Mark's count was wrong.

Seth wished real life worked like those two-handed automatic pistol scenes in the movies, or that he could fire with uncanny accuracy while managing to twist around and levitate at the same time. No such luck. He took shots at the zombies coming up on his right, hitting one in the head and winging the other in the shoulder, which just made the creature mad. The zombies on the left were fast shamblers, and Seth smelled them coming as they closed the distance.

One of them grabbed for him, sinking its bony fingers into Seth's bicep and jerking him toward a wide mouth full of teeth. Seth brought the gun up and fired, getting the zombie in the face. It let go and fell backward, but its buddy wasn't deterred at all and went for the waist, football tackle style.

That took Seth off balance, and they fell into the high grass. Zombies weren't super fast or very smart, but they were uncannily strong. One rotting hand pinned Seth's gun wrist to the ground, while the other went for his throat—again. Seth was lying on top of the sledgehammer, which dug into his side and might well have been a mile away for all that he could reach it. He made a fist and clocked the creature in the jaw, making it rear back and loosening its grip.

Gasping for air, Seth brought his knees up, unseating the zombie from astride him and kicked. The zombie fell on its ass, and Seth fired, putting a bullet between its eyes.

Strong arms grabbed Seth from behind, as teeth sank into his left shoulder. The wounded zombie had crawled closer during his tussle with the other two and seemed far more interested in Seth than in what remained of the raw chicken.

The bite hurt like a mofo, and Seth bit back a yelp. He slammed his head backward, into the zombie's face, and felt a satisfying crunch that wasn't his own skull. Seth turned his machete in his grip, so the knife faced backward and stabbed blindly, sinking the knife deep into zombie guts. The smell made his eyes water, but the zombie withdrew its teeth. Seth brought his fist down, hard, on the arm still holding him by the waist, and heard bones snap. He turned and fired, point blank, closing his eyes against the spattering gore.

"Nine," he yelled. "Nine—not six! Nine!" Not that Mark could hear him.

Seth used his machete to sever the heads, and the sledge-hammer to crush the skulls, but decided the chance of starting a wildfire was too high to set the bodies on fire. Covered in zombie guts, he made his way back to the motorcycle, grumbling all the way.

A small freshwater pond in front of the chalet looked cleaner than he was, so Seth did his best to rinse away the goop in the icy cold water, although nothing would bleach the images from his brain. He scraped away the worst from his shirt and jeans, scrubbed his short hair, washed off his weapons, and hoped that he didn't look like he just came from a massacre.

When he got back to the bike, he checked his phone. Ten missed calls or unread messages from Evan. He closed his eyes, took a deep breath, and steadied his courage.

That conversation he had been dreading had just gotten a lot worse.

5

EVAN

EVAN HAD READ SETH'S NOTE TWICE BEFORE THE MEANING SANK in. Seth had gone on a hunt without him, and since Evan hadn't yet mastered unhitching the fifth-wheeler to drive the pickup, that left him stranded, unable to help with the fight or even get to Seth if he got hurt and couldn't ride the bike home.

"You stupid, fucking, dumbass, stubborn asshole!" he raged to the empty trailer, crumpling the note and hurling it across the living room. Evan kicked a trash can and slammed a door, but nothing really let off the anger he felt.

He doesn't trust me to have his back. I've gotten lucky twice, but it wasn't skill as much as chance. Seth's afraid that one of these times, my luck will run out, and I'll be a liability. Shit. He's right. I've got to up my game, or someday, I'll be the reason he gets killed.

Evan needed to burn off his fury and think through the problem. He pulled on sweats and sneakers, grabbed his key to the trailer, and went out for a run. Along the way, he vaulted bike racks and picnic tables, jumped over gullies and railings, and outlined his own parkour route, pushing himself to his limits.

It was all so overwhelming. Zombies and witches were

real. His old life had gone down in flames, and his new life was uncertain, full of possibilities but nothing solid. He felt sure of his feelings for Seth, but now he worried that Seth might not be fully committed, or having second thoughts. There was so much to learn about hunting, lore, weapons, and magic, and he wondered whether he was up to the task. And the new business was exciting and stressful, but still hardly off the ground.

At the moment, Evan felt like he was trapped beneath a waterfall, drowning and unable to break free of the current.

Jump, dodge, run, climb. He ran until his lungs burned and his legs felt like jelly. No one in the nearly empty campground even noticed. Finally, he threw himself down on the brown grass next to the small fishing pond and tried to take comfort in watching the geese, but they flew away at his intrusion, leaving him alone.

Fuck. I've got to get a grip. I made a plan. Need to work the plan. If I work my plan, things will turn out. Maybe. God, I hope so.

Evan had realized right away that he needed more training than he could ask from Seth, so he'd gone looking for online videos on everything from strength training workouts to marksmanship tips. He watched a few whenever Seth was running errands or working outside. There really wasn't a reason for him to keep the videos secret, except that he didn't want Seth to be reminded of just how much Evan had to learn to keep up. Maybe if he worked hard enough, he could win Seth's trust.

He made his way back to the RV slower than he had begun, limping a bit from turning an ankle on a clumsy landing. Sweat plastered his hair to his face and ran down beneath his shirt. Evan looked around when he got to the trailer, hoping Seth had returned, but neither the bike nor his boyfriend was in sight.

With a sigh, Evan let himself in, locked the door behind him and set the security system, and then showered and changed. He checked his phone, hoping to see a missed call or message, to no avail.

He said he needed to "take care of something." That doesn't have to mean he went on a hunt. Maybe we needed supplies, or he went to meet someone who had details about the Pittsburgh warlock. But deep inside, his intuition told him that Seth hadn't just gone to the store. Evan weighed whether or not to call, then gave in and dialed. He wasn't surprised when the call went to voicemail.

"Seth—whatever you're doing, be careful. We need to talk. We can work this out. Just…come back safe, and we'll figure everything out together."

He ended the call and leaned back against the wall, closing his eyes. Evan tried to still his worry—about Seth's safety, their relationship, the new business, hunting, everything—but didn't completely succeed.

Too restless to read or watch TV, and too tired to do another workout, Evan settled in at the table with his laptop and opened his email. He was pleased to see several new requests for estimates from people who had found his website, as well as payment notices from a couple of clients for whom he'd already done small projects.

Then he saw another email, from one of his very first customers. *"Evan, you did such a great job on our project, we'd like to talk to you about working for us full time in our Richmond office. We can offer you a competitive salary and benefits. Please call to arrange an interview."*

Evan stared at the message as his heart thudded. He had liked the client when they talked on the phone, and the company—a local firm specializing in eco-friendly workout gear—intrigued him. Suddenly, the opportunity that eluded him for so long—a real job that would put his degree, interests, and talent to good use—sat waiting to be claimed in his inbox.

And all he'd have to do was give up Seth.

Evan paced, trying to still his racing thoughts. Watching videos didn't distract him, and going through several free weights routines did nothing to ease his tension. He veered between worry and anger, as he tried and failed to get an answer from Seth.

What if he's injured, and no one knows where he is? How the hell are we going to work this out if he won't trust me? Maybe he's just gone to research the next hunt. What the fuck does he think he's doing, walking out like that?

His heart thudded when he heard the Hayabusa pull in beside the trailer, but he stayed back, unwilling to run to the door like a love-struck teenager, and uncertain whether if he did, he'd greet Seth with a kiss or a kick.

The delay between when the bike's motor stilled and when Evan heard Seth's key in the door worried him, and he went to disarm the security. He could not cover his gasp at Seth's appearance.

Seth's jacket, shirt, and jeans were torn and gouged. A bloody bite—it looked human—marked Seth's shoulder too close for comfort to his jugular. His lips were blue, and he was shaking so hard he dropped his keys. He stank like week-old roadkill.

"What happened?" Evan moved to help Seth retrieve his keys, then eased him out of his ruined jacket. Their argument could wait—right now, Seth needed his help.

"Zombies," Seth managed through chattering teeth. "Mark can't count."

Whatever that meant. "Okay," Evan said, drawing out the syllables. He eyed Seth from head to toe. "Those chunks will stop up the water system," he said, having gained an understanding of how the trailer's plumbing worked. "We're going to the bathhouse." He left Seth for a moment to grab supplies —towels and fresh clothing, as well as soap, shampoo, and jackets for both of them.

"I'm sorry," Seth said miserably, his voice trembling as he

shook with cold. "I fucked up. Shouldn't have left without you. I'm so sorry—"

Evan slung an arm around Seth's waist to keep him on his feet as they made the short trek to the campground bath-house. Only a couple of other trailers were at the park, and Evan doubted their owners used the communal changing rooms and showers at this time of year. But with a small indoor pool connected, the park's owners kept the bathhouse open year-round. The building was warm, and each of the large individual showers were shielded by opaque curtains. Just in case, Evan locked the main door from the inside to assure privacy.

He steered Seth toward the shower and tried to hold his breath. "You can tell me all about it when you're warm."

"I didn't want to wake you," Seth mumbled as Evan stripped him. "I was afraid of what you were going to say." Seth looked too cold and miserable to attempt any flirting as Evan peeled away the last of his clothing. The bite on his shoulder was already red and puffy, and Evan didn't want to think too much about what kind of infection a zombie bite could cause. Except—

"Shit. The bite. You're not going to turn all 'bra-aaaa-ins' are you?"

Seth shook his head. "That only happens…on TV." He was shaking so hard, his words were slurred. Evan turned on the shower, making sure the water was warm but not too hot and maneuvered Seth under the spray. He slipped out of his own clothes and joined Seth in the shower.

"You're an asshole," Evan muttered, soaping up his hands and running them over Seth's body. He no longer smelled the stink, which probably meant his nose wasn't working right. "What the hell did you think you were doing, leaving me here like that?" His words lacked heat. He still felt angry, but the reality of Seth's close call made him feel tangled up inside.

"You're new at this," Seth replied quietly, barely audible

above the sound of the water. "Been pushing you hard. Thought you could rest up. Wasn't supposed to be a hard hunt."

"Yeah, well. Didn't work that way, did it? You could have gotten killed," Evan grated, taking extra care with the tender skin around the bite. Christ, the zombie had ripped some of the flesh, and the bite had been deep. He'd need to clean it with alcohol and use the salve Seth showed him that was both medical and magical. Somewhere there had to be some antibiotics.

"That's the life. Hunters get killed. Like cops, or soldiers. For a cause."

Seth sounded exhausted. He bent his head for Evan to shampoo the gunk from his hair, and as Evan ran his hands through the blond spikes, he felt his body debate between fucking and fighting.

God, it felt like they'd been at odds forever, though it was only two days. Evan's gaze came back to the bite on Seth's shoulder, and his mind supplied the scenario that let a zombie get close enough to nearly rip out his throat. The shiver that went through Evan's body had nothing to do with the cold.

I could have lost him, and I wouldn't even have known where to find the body. The mix of fear and anticipated grief felt like a shiv to his heart.

Evan pressed up against Seth's back, arms around his waist. "If we're going to do this, then we need to be a team. You don't get to run off and be a hero on your own."

"Sorry," Seth mumbled.

Despite his jumbled emotions, Evan's body clearly had ideas of its own, and his cock filled as it pressed up against Seth's naked ass. He reached around to find Seth just as hard and closed his hand around Seth's prick.

"Need you," Seth groaned, as Evan began to work him, a little rough with frustration and the aftermath of fear. Evan rutted against Seth, sliding between the muscular globes of his ass, not quite ready for a true fucking until the air was cleared between them. This...this was letting off steam and confirming that Seth had come back to him, alive. So if Evan jerked him harder than usual, Seth accepted the penance, and Evan took his lover's submission as a form of apology.

"Gonna come," Seth gasped. Evan gripped Seth's hip tightly with his left hand, pulling them flush together, while he let his thumb catch that sensitive spot beneath the head, then swipe over the slit. Seth cried out Evan's name and shot, and Evan followed seconds later, coating Seth's back and ass with his spend.

Seth leaned forward, supporting himself with both hands against the shower wall, and Evan leaned over him, as they let the water sluice away the evidence of their orgasms. Only then did Evan realize that the shower had cooled.

"Time to get out," Evan said with a chuckle. "Or you'll get frozen all over again." He shut off the water, then left Seth leaning against the wall while he reached for two towels. Evan stayed close as they toweled off, not sure Seth was steady enough on his feet alone.

He went to the locker room and returned with sweatpants and t-shirts for both of them, and settled the jacket over Seth's shoulder since he didn't want to aggravate his injury. They made their way back to the trailer, after Evan has assured that no zombie gobbets remained to give the cleaning crew a heart attack. Once they were back inside, Evan led Seth to the table, grabbing their medical kit on the way.

"Sit. That bite looks nasty."

"Can't believe I let one of them get behind me," Seth grumbled. Evan pushed his computer out of the way as he sat Seth down and got out the supplies.

"That's why you need a wingman," Evan chided. Maybe he should be angrier, but the day's worry and Seth's injury drained it out of him. Yes, they had a lot to talk about, to work out. Given how new—and complicated—their relationship was, that hardly seemed like a surprise. But maybe, if they stood their ground, they'd have the time to figure things out.

"We're almost out of antibiotics," Evan said, rattling what remained in the prescription bottle he found in the cabinet. "Better find a source to get some more." He handed a glass of water and a tablet to Seth, who downed them in silence.

"Mail-order veterinary supply house," Seth mumbled. "Fish antibiotics work just fine."

"Nice to know. Let me get this cleaned and treated," Evan said, daubing at the torn skin with alcohol pads. Seth hissed at the burn. Moments later, the wound was covered in salve and bandaged, and Evan went to wash up.

"So...are you going?" Seth asked. His voice sounded tired and empty.

Evan turned. "Going where?"

Seth pointed to Evan's computer, and Evan felt his stomach drop. He'd left the email open with the job offer, practically in front of Seth's face.

"That just came this afternoon," he stammered.

Seth closed his eyes and let out a long breath. "Maybe you should take it. Sounds like a good deal. And...you'd be safe."

Evan's anger spiked. "You want me to go?"

Seth shook his head. "No. But I'm selfish. I should want what's best for you. And that isn't me." The pain and resignation in his voice made Evan's throat tighten.

"And what if I disagree?" Evan challenged. "What if I think we're too good together to give up?" He threw his hands in the air, struggling for words. "Look, I never thought I'd be fighting monsters and running from the cops, hunting for crazy, undead warlocks. Shit—that sounds even worse out loud." Evan turned, pacing the living room.

"But I've never felt this way about anyone before," he continued, desperate to make Seth understand. "I can't stand the thought of leaving you. And today, when I didn't know where you were or if you were all right—"

"I'm sorry," Seth said, his voice a low rasp.

"I couldn't think straight, worrying. And I got that email and tried it on for size in my mind. It's everything I thought I wanted. Except, I couldn't have it and you. That's when I realized that the job wasn't enough." He moved to meet Seth's gaze. "I want this. Us. I want to fight beside you and fuck you and figure things out together. But you've got to trust me, man. Gotta work with me."

Seth looked away, chagrinned. "I want us, too. I'm just so afraid you'll realize that this is all a mistake and you can do better."

"I—" Evan started, but Seth kept on like he hadn't heard.

"When that guy in the bar hit on you, I wanted to punch his lights out," Seth admitted. "Not because I really thought you'd cheat on me. I didn't. But because I saw how easy it would be for you to trade up."

"Obviously, we need to work on your self-image," Evan said, resorting to gentle snark to lighten the moment. "And I reacted like I did because Mike used to get real jealous over stupid things, right before he—" Evan hadn't shared all the details about his abusive stalker ex, but Seth knew enough to fill in the blanks.

"That's not who I am," Seth said in a low, quiet voice. "I'm scared to death that my mistake on a hunt might get you killed, but I will never do anything to hurt you. I swear."

Evan closed the laptop and slid it away, then took both Seth's hands in his. "I believe you. And I knew that. But…old reactions are hard to get rid of."

"Can we pick up where we left off?" Seth asked, and Evan saw a vulnerability in his eyes that he usually only glimpsed in the midst of making love.

"Pretty sure that's what we're doing right now," Evan said, then he moved forward and kissed Seth on the lips. Seth leaned in, and the kiss turned tender, full of longing and unspoken need. When they finally broke apart, both of them were flushed, pupils blown, looking a bit twitterpated.

"Okay, yeah?" Seth asked.

"Yeah," Evan confirmed. His body wanted more, already recovered from the quickie in the shower, but he saw exhaustion in the line of Seth's shoulders and worried that the bite hurt more than his lover let on.

"Let me fix you a sandwich, and then we're going to bed."

"Promise?" Tired as he was, Seth managed a lecherous grin.

"Count on it."

6

SETH

EVAN REFUSED TO EVEN DISCUSS ANOTHER HUNT UNTIL THE BITE on Seth's shoulder stopped looking infected and began to heal. Since Seth knew he screwed up big-time, in more ways than one, he didn't push to move on, although he did try to convince his boyfriend that letting Seth fuck him would speed up the healing process.

Or the reverse. Seth was fine with that, too.

Frustratingly, Evan refused to be swayed until Seth could put his full weight on his injured shoulder, although they found plenty of other ways to burn off cabin fever while Seth recuperated. Several days of hand jobs, blow jobs, and frot took the edge off, but Seth was ready for makeup sex. More than that, he just wanted to feel like he and Evan were fully reconnected.

"Even people who don't meet each other in a gunfight have arguments now and again," Evan told him as he changed the dressing on the wound. "I think it goes with the whole relationship territory."

"Arguing sucks," Seth pouted.

"Well then, all the more reason not to have more of them than necessary." Evan taped the last piece of gauze and leaned back to admire his handiwork. "I think I'm gonna add some field medic videos to my playlist," he mused.

"Probably not a bad idea," Seth agreed. While he recuperated, Evan had shown him the weaponry and training videos he'd been watching. Seth, eager for something to pass the time, watched with him, pointing out details pro and con from his own experience.

The shoulder still throbbed. Seth chafed at being taken care of, even as he found himself enjoying the attention. Had their situations been reversed, he would have fussed over Evan, needing to restrain himself from just rolling Evan in bubble wrap to prevent future injuries.

On the other hand, naked bubble wrap rolling might be fun.

"Are you even listening to me?" Evan asked, canting his head in mock annoyance.

"Yes, dear," Seth teased, wondering where he could get large enough sheets of bubble wrap.

Evan rolled his eyes. "When your shoulder is back at one hundred percent, I want you to teach me to drive the Hayabusa."

Seth stared at him. "Seriously? You don't even like the bike."

Evan shrugged. "I'm learning to like it. Won't say I want to go off-roading—"

"Not with my bike!"

"But I need to know how to drive in a pinch. What if you got hurt? What if you took the truck and I needed to get somewhere?" He paused. "Speaking of which, I also need to know how to couple and uncouple the truck and the fifth-wheeler. And I want to practice driving the truck. I haven't driven anything bigger than my old Camaro." Which had also gotten destroyed in the apartment fire.

If Seth needed more reassurance that Evan intended to stay, having him volunteer to learn how to drive the truck and the motorcycle definitely made his case. "You're right. I should have offered before this. It's just—"

"We're figuring it out as we go," Evan replied.

Seth hadn't asked again about the job offer, but Evan told him, unprompted, that he had turned the opportunity down. "Maybe someday, when we've stopped the warlocks, we can think about staying in one place," Evan had said, off-handedly picturing a distant future Seth wanted so badly it ached. "For now, I'm kinda excited about seeing more of the country."

"We don't exactly hit the top tourist spots," Seth observed.

"I prefer to think of it as being off the beaten path."

Seth's phone buzzed. Evan scooped it up before Seth could respond. "Hi, Toby. Yes, he's here. But he hasn't recovered yet from that 'easy' zombie hunt." Evan's tone carried a bit of a dig as he gave Seth the side-eye, and Seth figured he deserved it.

Seth couldn't hear Toby's next comments, but he read the expression on Evan's face loud and clear. "Toby, is Seth the only hunter you guys know? I mean, what about that Mark guy Seth talks about?" He listened for a moment. "Oh, you called him first? No one else close, huh. Okay. And it can't wait?" His face darkened. "Shit. Then lay it on me."

"Put him on speaker," Seth urged. Evan grimaced, then pressed the screen and Toby's voice came through, loud and clear.

"Look, I'm sorry about the timing," Toby said. "But I got wind of trouble with what I think are kobolds a couple of hours away from you guys, and I don't have anyone else in the area who could handle it. I *am* trying to connect with more hunters, honest. But you know how it is. Everyone's skittish about having anyone know too much about where they're going or what they're doing. So it takes a while to build a network."

"I get it," Seth said. Evan gave a huff of annoyance but settled next to Seth to hear what came next.

"Kobolds, huh. Nasty little mine spirits," Seth mused. "Where are they?"

"Centralia."

Evan frowned. "Isn't that the town where the coal mines caught on fire?"

"Yep," Toby confirmed. "And it's almost completely abandoned, thanks to the fire that probably won't burn itself out for a century. But kobolds like fire, and every so often, someone has to go in and clean them out before they become a hazard."

"To whom?" Evan asked. "I mean, Centralia's a ghost town."

"Not completely," Toby said. "But the people who still live there have more to worry about than kobolds, and it's their choice to stick around. We've heard reports that the kobolds are moving through some of the other abandoned mines in the area, toward populated places. Had an incident at a mine museum not far from there. No one got hurt, and it was just one kobold, but it could have been ugly. A guy who lives there called a friend of a friend of mine, which is why I'm calling you. He'll be your contact in town, run interference to keep the cops away."

"I didn't think it was ever just one kobold," Seth replied. "Don't they travel in packs?"

"Usually. Which is why we try to monitor the situation and keep the pack size small." Toby sounded tired, and Seth figured that playing central dispatch to a bunch of overly independent hunters probably took a toll.

"You're not expecting us to go into a mine that's on fire to hunt these things, right?" Evan's voice had taken on an edge.

"Contrary to appearances, I'm not trying to kill you," Toby replied. "Really, I'm not," he added as if he sensed Evan's wariness. "Of course you don't go into the mines.

Aside from the bad air and the fire part, no one who knows what they're doing ever goes in after one of those little fuckers. Gotta make them come to you."

"Yeah, tried that with the zombies Mark sent me after, and it worked a little too well," Seth replied ruefully, wincing as he shifted his sore shoulder.

"Kobolds like sweets, so a cake or a bunch of cupcakes makes a good lure," Toby said. "Also, fresh cream and they're fond of decent beer."

"Who isn't?" Seth mused, earning a glare from Evan, who smacked him lightly on his good shoulder.

"And of all things, roast chicken," Toby added.

"So we lure them out with a picnic, and then what?" Evan asked. Seth noticed Evan had started to get picky about the fine points, and couldn't blame him. In what they did, the devil—literally—could be in the details.

"You have an AK?" Toby asked like it was the most natural question in the world. Evan turned to stare at Seth, with a raised eyebrow.

"No. Lots of ammo for shotguns and handguns, though. And my Glock shoots plenty fast unless we're talking about facing down a friggin' army."

"That works," Toby said. "There won't be an army of them, but more than a few, that's for sure."

"They're fey, aren't they?" Seth asked. "So iron should work. And if we spill something with small grains—rice, sugar, salt—they have to stop and count them, right?"

"In theory," Toby agreed. "I wouldn't stake my life on them being too OCD to go after fresh meat."

"Give us a minute," Seth said and put the phone on mute. He turned to Evan. "Okay, partner. What do you think?" He saw the spark in Evan's eyes at the realization that they were going to make the decision together.

"Are you up for it? The truth."

Seth flexed his shoulder muscles. The injury twinged but

had otherwise healed up. "Yeah. I am. You want to do this? 'Cause if you don't, we can say no."

Evan looked like he was debating the question internally for a moment and then nodded. "I'm not going to get better without practice, and we've got a warlock to kill once we get to Pittsburgh."

Seth unmuted the call. "Yeah, we're in. And so help me God, you'd better be able to count right."

THE DRIVE TO CENTRALIA TOOK JUST UNDER FOUR HOURS. THEY took the truck, and Seth gave Evan a driving lesson on the way since they left the RV at the campground. To Seth's relief, the tension between them was gone, and while he had no illusions that they had figured everything out, at least they'd made it through their first real fight.

The late November day grew overcast, threatening rain. Seth and Evan left the Turnpike and angled north on smaller roads, finally ending up on Route 61 headed for Centralia.

"Offhand, I feel a little unwelcome," Evan said, nodding toward one of the many signs they passed warning them about dangerous conditions, toxic gasses, and possible mine subsidence.

"People still live in Centralia. Not many, but some," Seth said. "This isn't the only highway that goes through there. The roads just got routed around where the damage is the worst."

They grabbed some gas masks when they stowed the rest of their gear, just in case. A cooler held the cream, beer, roast chicken, and cupcakes, while Seth's bag now had containers of sugar and rice along with the salt. They had plenty of iron ammo as well as knives. Still, Seth felt antsy. He hoped Toby's information was right, and that he hadn't just led them into another ambush.

"Hey, we'll take it as it comes, all right?" Evan said with a faint smile as if he guessed the direction of Seth's thoughts. Then he reached over and gave Seth's thigh a squeeze, high up, so his fingers slipped into the crotch of Seth's jeans.

"You're gonna wreck us if you keep that up," Seth warned, but he was smiling.

"Just a promise of what you can look forward to if we both come out relatively unscathed," Evan replied with a naughty grin.

The weather had turned colder, and mist rose all around them. A weathered *"Welcome to Centralia"* sign looked less than sincere, especially with a wrecked and rusted Jeep in the weeds nearby. An eerie quiet settled over them as they drove slowly past deserted houses left to fall into disrepair, and shuttered businesses that would never reopen. A torn and faded awning hung in strips from its wire frame above the door to the permanently-closed cafe, next to a defunct clothing store and a darkened jewelry shop.

All that remained of some houses were concrete steps to nowhere or a crumbling brick foundation. Nature seemed to be taking care of the rest, as the damage of storms and falling branches broke windows and collapsed roofs.

Seth had set his GPS for the source of the disturbance, near the entrance to the mine where the fire started. Those roads were blocked with sawhorses and signs, warning curious explorers to turn back. Seth parked the truck, and they got out, with Seth shouldering the duffel and Evan carrying the cooler. The late November wind carried a bite, but the warmth of Centralia's underground fires made fog rise from the split pavement.

"I swear this all looks familiar," Evan said, glancing from one side to another. "I've been here."

"Really?"

"I know this street," Evan said. He pointed ahead of them, toward the edge of town. "There's going to be a hospital on one side, and a school on the other. And—" His eyes widened. "Oh, shit. I know why this looks familiar. It's Silent Hill."

"What?" Seth wracked his brain to make the connection, and all he came up with was a vague memory of playing video games with his brother, Jesse.

"It was a series of video games and a movie, back when I was a kid," Evan said. "Set in an abandoned town where monsters were real. Later on, I read that they based the look of the town of Silent Hill on a real place—Centralia." He shivered. "One thing I remember—we really don't want to go into that hospital."

As they walked on, Seth got some flashes of déjà vu he attributed to the same long-forgotten video game. He pushed those thoughts aside, needing to keep his mind on the hunt. When they reached the location where Toby had sent them to meet their contact, all they saw was a stretch of cracked asphalt, split open in some places all the way down to the gravel beneath.

"So, where is he?" Evan demanded.

"I don't know, but someone's coming," Seth replied quietly, with a nod toward the dark shape just becoming visible in the fog. He reached behind him and drew his Glock, keeping it out of sight.

"You must be the ones Toby sent." The man who stepped out of the mist looked to be in his seventies, still standing ramrod tall, with a ropy build that suggested a lifetime of hard, physical work. Unkempt white hair poked from beneath the edges of his trucker's cap. His lined face showed his age, but the blue eyes that met Seth's were sharp and uncompromising. "I'm George," he added, offering his hand first to Seth and then to Evan. "I swear you hunters get younger every year."

Seth found himself squaring his shoulders and drawing

up to his full height. "Toby said you could show us a good place to set the trap and make sure we aren't interrupted."

George chuckled. "Did he, now? Well, then, come on." He gestured for them to follow him. Evan exchanged a questioning glance with Seth, who shrugged and then nodded, falling in behind their guide.

"Lived here in Centralia all my life, thanks for asking," George said. "Used to be a nice town. Real friendly. Civic pride. Then the mines caught fire, and it all went straight to hell."

The farther they walked along the cracked and twisted asphalt, the stronger the smell of coal smoke became. A faint, sporadic beep came from the phone-sized carbon dioxide monitor on Seth's belt, a last-minute inspiration he'd picked up at the hardware store. George seemed none the worse for the wear, but the smoke was already starting to give Seth a headache, and from the way Evan pinched the bridge of his nose, it bothered him, too. The air burned in Seth's throat, and his chest felt tight. All the more reason to get done and get gone.

"I don't think any of the residents are going to bother you out here," George said, finally stopping a little way past the abandoned hospital. "No one comes this way anymore. No reason to. Air's worse, and there's nothing anyone needs 'round this end of town." He shrugged. "Naught out here but the mine, and nothing good's come of *it* in over fifty years."

"What about the police?" Evan asked.

"State Troopers come by now and again to scare off vandals, but the local cops packed up and left town with the rest of the folks," George replied. "All but a few stubborn old codgers like me. And soon enough, we'll be gone, too." He coughed, a deep hacking sound. Seth couldn't help wondering if it was from working the mines, being a lifelong smoker, or enduring Centralia's hellish fumes.

George waved at the road ahead of him while he struggled for breath, indicating that they'd come to the place for the trap. Seth squinted into the distance, trying to figure out where the mine entrance had been, but the fog shrouded everything too thickly for him to get his bearings.

"I'll make sure none of the locals interfere, not that they'd be so inclined," George wheezed. Seth figured that was the old man's face-saving excuse to leave before the fighting started, and he watched George vanish into the mist.

Seth made sure both he and Evan had their handguns and knives. They put on their gas masks, since Seth wasn't willing to have a coughing fit when he needed to be aiming and shooting. He grabbed the salt, sugar, and rice and cast the grains in a wide circle, thickly enough to cover the asphalt. Then he stepped back to get the rest of the weapons ready, as Evan moved to set the trap.

"See if you can find us some steel pipe," Evan called to him, pulling his mask away a few inches to be able to speak. "And set the sledgehammer out."

Seth gave him a look. "Why?"

"I remember those did well in the game. Maybe the designer drew from real life."

Finding two lengths of pipe wasn't difficult, and Seth set them out next to the long-handled sledgehammer they usually carried for emergencies. "Got it."

Evan walked carefully into the center of the grain-strewn area, bending to set out the chicken and cupcakes. He placed a six-pack of beer nearby, next to a bowl he filled with cream. Then he carefully backtracked to where Seth waited, shotgun in one hand, Glock in the other.

"Do we have to call their name three times and turn around?" Evan quipped. Seth knew his partner covered fear with sarcasm.

"No, I think they'll figure it out on their own," Seth said. A scrabbling sound came from the direction of the mine entrance, like the sound of hard boots—or claws—on asphalt.

Seth and Evan drew back into the fog so as not to alert the kobolds to their presence.

The sound of his own breathing through the gas mask added to the creepiness of their surroundings, and Seth imagined that he could hear the beating of his own heart. The scrabbling noise grew louder, sending a chill down his spine as the kobolds came closer.

Evan startled when the first of the creatures came into view. Seth laid a hand on his arm to keep him from moving forward. The kobold wasn't cute like a garden gnome, or pretty like the fairies in picture books. It stood perhaps four feet tall, with blue-gray skin and patches of wiry gray hair on an otherwise bald head. The kobold's square jaws looked powerful, and while he wasn't tall, the tunic-clad body had plenty of lean muscle.

The creature scented the air, and its mouth parted, revealing a row of sharp teeth behind thin, red lips. It squinted in their direction, peering through the fog, but did not seem alarmed. Seth wondered how well kobold senses worked aboveground. Then the kobold gave a shrill whistle, and a dozen of its friends broke through the mist.

"Shit," Evan murmured, barely above a whisper. He tensed, gripping his guns tightly.

"Wait for it," Seth replied, just as quietly.

The kobolds descended on the bait like starving piranha, fighting over the chicken as they tore the carcass to pieces, pulling the six-pack back and forth in a tug-of-war, and spilling the cream as they struggled to claim the bowl for themselves.

"Now!" Seth hissed. He and Evan opened fire. The kobolds shrieked, but every time one tried to run, it did not seem to be able to leave the area within the trap.

Bullets hit, but the kobolds didn't go down. "What the hell?" Seth yelped.

"Keep firing!" Evan shouted above the noise of the

gunfire. "Nothing in the game ever went down with just one shot."

Seth had never figured he'd be taking monster-hunting lessons from a decade-old video game, but he kept on shooting. Some of the rounds bounced off hide that must have been tougher than a rhino's. Soon enough, Seth worked out the weak points and changed his aim. He and Evan kept up a constant barrage, covering each other as they reloaded, alternating between their Glocks and shotguns. It sounded like a war zone. Gradually, the number of kobolds standing dwindled.

"That's the last one." Evan's voice was muffled beneath his mask.

Seth's battle sense remained on high alert, and he edged closer to the trap, counting bodies.

"We're missing two—"

Before he could finish his sentence, the missing kobolds were on them. One of the creatures launched itself at Seth, leaping at him from the front and sinking its claws into Seth's barely-healed shoulder.

Seth fired on automatic at close range, and the kobold fell backward, then lay still on the cracked pavement. He searched the fog for Evan. "Evan!"

Evan's response was a yelp, and Seth went running. His Glock was out of ammo, and there wasn't time to reload, so he shoved it into his waistband and brought up his shotgun.

A kobold had Evan pinned to the ground, far too close for Seth to get in a safe shot. Despite their height difference and Evan's fierce struggle, the kobold kept Evan down. Strong, clawed hands locked around Evan's wrists, as the toothy maw got closer to this throat.

Evan's gun lay several feet away where the creature knocked it from his hand. Nearby lay his length of steel pipe. Seth set down the shotgun, grabbed the pipe with both hands, and ran forward.

"Batter up!" he shouted, swinging for the fences. The steel pipe connected with a body that felt more like granite than flesh, sending a jolt through both of Seth's arms. Still, the blow took the kobold's attention off Evan and focused it on Seth, which he counted as a win.

"Get the hell away from him," Seth growled, holding the pipe at the ready for the creature to attack. Evan scrambled to his feet, then vanished in the fog.

Before the kobold could strike, it suddenly flew sideways, off its feet, to land in a heap on the cracked street. Evan held the long-handled sledgehammer with both hands, his breath rasping, Vader-like, through his mask. He shot Seth a thumb's up.

Just then, a new figure appeared, silhouetted in the fog, snuffling and wheezing. Seth grabbed his shotgun but kept the pipe in his left hand. Evan retrieved his Glock, still holding the sledgehammer for backup.

George emerged from the mist, coughing like he'd bring up a lung. "Looks like you got them," he said with a nod as if they'd cleaned out an infestation of squirrels from the attic.

"What do we do with them?" Seth asked. "They like fire, and they like being underground, so burning or burying the bodies probably isn't a good idea."

George nodded, thinking it over. "There's a pond out past the municipal building. I'll bring my truck and some shovels. We'll haul them out there, and dump them in. Not like the water's gonna get any more polluted than it is already."

They drove back to the trailer in exhausted silence. Seth had made sure neither of their injuries were more serious than scrapes or bruises, although the image of the kobold with its sharp teeth looming over Evan's throat would haunt his nightmares for a long time. Evan huddled in the passenger seat of the truck despite the heater at full blast, looking shaken and weary.

After driving for half an hour with Evan staring out the window, Seth cleared his throat. "So...your video-fu saved the day," he said. "Good call."

Evan managed a smile that didn't reach his eyes. "All the hours I spent playing those games had to be good for something."

"You held it together and handled the situation," Seth said, wanting Evan to know how much he valued having a partner in every sense. "I was impressed."

"You were no slouch yourself," Evan replied. "We make a good team."

"I think I'm going to add Kevlar vests to the supply list," Seth said. "We might not be getting shot at, but those claws are a bitch."

When they reached the trailer, a hot shower was the first thing on the agenda. By then, Seth's "good" shoulder was starting to turn purple from the kobold's grip, and so were Evan's ribs, where the creature had pinned him with its surprising weight. They opted for the bathhouse again, taking supplies with them. Under the warm water, their hands moved tenderly over each other, soaping away the sweat, sliding along unbroken skin to reassure that the injuries weren't worse, verifying that they were both whole and relatively undamaged.

Evan sank to his knees, sparing a glance upward through wet lashes before he swallowed Seth down. Seth braced himself against the shower walls, and let his head fall forward as Evan let his tongue swirl over Seth's hard length and tease at his slit, before taking him to the back of his throat.

"Not gonna last," Seth warned. Evan squeezed his ass, teasing at his crack with one finger, letting him know wordlessly that this wasn't a marathon tonight. Seth came hard, and Evan pulled him close, continuing to suck and bob until

Seth was completely spent. Seth leaned bonelessly against the shower wall as Evan rose, looking a little pleased with himself, then leaned in for a kiss. Seth tasted himself on Evan's lips.

"My turn," Seth said when Evan pulled back.

"I'll take a raincheck," Evan said. "I don't think my ribs could take much heavy breathing right now. Maybe in the morning?" He gave Seth another kiss, and they turned off the water, sliding past each other to towel off. They hurried back to the trailer, bracing against the cold walk from the bathhouse. Once inside, Seth held out his hand, leading Evan to the bedroom, curling around him beneath the covers.

I'm so lucky to have him. I can't believe he's mine, Seth thought as he drifted off to sleep, content.

In the morning, Evan was gone.

Seth woke with a start and realized the spot beside him was cold and empty. He listened for sounds in the bathroom, but the trailer was eerily quiet.

"Evan?" he called out, thinking his lover had gone to the kitchen to start breakfast. But when he walked into the living area, Evan was nowhere to be seen. That's when Seth realized two things. Evan's wallet was gone. So were the keys to the truck.

Seth leaned against the kitchen counter and tried to will his heart to stop racing. His breath came fast and short as he tried and failed to find a reason for Evan's absence.

"There's got to be a note," he said, retracing his steps to the bedroom, but found nothing on the nightstand. Out in the kitchen, the counter was empty, and there was nothing tacked onto the fridge.

"Fuck," Seth said, dropping into a seat at the table. He argued with himself that there was a perfectly logical explanation. That Evan had just run out for milk. But Evan had never gone off to the store by himself before, especially not driving the truck, which was still new to him.

Seth's shoulders slumped, and he rested his head in his hands. *Maybe it was just too much for him. One monster after another—no one sane lives like this. I should have realized how much it bothered him.* He remembered how tender Evan had been in the shower the night before, every touch a caress. *Was he telling me good-bye?*

The rumble of the Silverado roused Seth from his thoughts, and he jumped to his feet. Before he could reach the door, Evan stumbled through, clutching heavy grocery bags. Something smelled wonderful.

"You're back," Seth said, not making any attempt to hide the relief in his voice.

Evan looked confused. "Yeah—I left a note. Maybe it fell off the counter. Said I had to run into town."

Seth followed him into the kitchen. Evan set his packages down, then stooped to pick up a piece of paper that had fallen to the floor. "See?"

Seth was still processing the fact that Evan had come back —he hadn't run away, hadn't had his fill of hunting. And...he brought back enough food for an army.

"What is all this?" Seth asked as he finally found his voice.

Evan grinned. "Thanksgiving dinner, you idiot. Or did you completely lose track of what day it is?"

Seth stared at him, gobsmacked. "I—"

"You did," Evan said with a chuckle. "You totally did. Luckily, the diner in town took online orders. Roast turkey, mashed potatoes and gravy, buttered corn, stuffing, and two kinds of homemade pie. All we need to do is pop it in the oven to heat it up, and *voila*! Instant Thanksgiving."

Relief, gratitude, and love flooded through Seth so strongly that he thought his knees might buckle. Evan was already turning on the oven and arranging the disposable metal catering pans to fit everything in at once. Seth waited until Evan had closed the oven door before he came up behind him and slipped his arms around Evan's waist.

"I was scared when I woke up, and you weren't here," he confessed, pressing his cheek against Evan's hair.

"Told you I'm not going anywhere without you," Evan replied, covering Seth's hands with his own. "Well, not farther than the diner, anyhow."

"I know. But, after everything—"

"After everything, I'm more sure than ever that this—here with you—is where I want to be," Evan said. He turned in Seth's arms, facing him and sliding his hands down to grip Seth's waist. "I love you, Seth Tanner. And after we stuff ourselves with this turkey, I've got plans for what else we can take turns stuffing," he added with a lecherous grin. "After all, you owe me a raincheck."

END

AFTERWORD

Thank you for reading *Burn*, and continuing the journey with Seth and Evan that started in *Witchbane*. Stay tuned, because there are a lot more adventures yet to come! *Dark Rivers* is the next novel, with more after that.

It takes a village to create a book. Many thanks to my beta readers, Amy, Andrea, Chris, Darrell, Donald, Laurie, and Mindy. Thanks also to my launch team (Lily, Karolina, Shauna, Anne 1, Cheryl, Jason, Sherrie, Kathryn, Lynn, Anne 2) and members of my Shadow Alliance and Worlds of Morgan Brice for helping spread the word about the books. And of course, thanks to awesome cover artist Lou Harper and to my editor and formatter, hubby Larry N. Martin.

If you enjoyed the cameo appearances by Mark Wojcik and Simon Kincaid—or wondered about Seth's comment concerning the contacts in Charleston who could get rid of cursed or haunted objects—they all have their own series! Simon Kincaid and Vic D'Amato are the main characters in my Badlands series (urban fantasy M/M paranormal romance). Cassidy Kincaide (Simon's cousin), Teag Logan, and Sorren are the Charleston contacts who specialize in neutralizing cursed and haunted objects, and you'll find them in my Deadly Curiosities series (urban fantasy, written under my Gail Z. Martin name). Mark Wojcik stars in the Spells, Salt, & Steel: New Templar Knights series, co-written with Larry N. Martin (snarky monster hunting adventure). Enjoy!

ABOUT THE AUTHOR

Morgan Brice is the romance pen name of bestselling author Gail Z. Martin. Morgan writes urban fantasy male/male paranormal romance, with plenty of action, adventure, and supernatural thrills to go with the happily ever after. Gail writes epic fantasy and urban fantasy, and together with co-author hubby Larry N. Martin, steampunk and comedic horror, all of which have less romance, and more explosions.

On the rare occasions Morgan isn't writing, she's either reading, cooking, or spoiling two very pampered dogs.

Watch for additional new series from Morgan Brice, and more books in the Witchbane and Badlands universes coming soon!

Where to find me, and how to stay in touch

On the web at https://morganbrice.com. Sign up for my newsletter and never miss a new release! http://eepurl.com/dy_8oL.

Facebook Group—The place for news about upcoming books, convention appearances, special fun like contests and giveaways, plus location photos, fantasy casting, and more! Look for The Worlds of Morgan Brice. facebook.com/groups/143333126341151

You can also find Morgan on Twitter: @MorganBriceBook and Pinterest (for Morgan and Gail): pinterest.com/Gzmartin.

∾

Support Indie Authors

When you support independent authors, you help influence what kind of books you'll see more of and what types of stories will be available, because the authors themselves decide which books to write, not a big publishing conglomerate. Independent authors are local creators, supporting their families with the books they produce. Thank you for supporting independent authors and small press fiction!

BOOKS BY MORGAN BRICE:

Witchbane Series

Witchbane

Burn, A Witchbane Novella

Dark Rivers - *Coming Soon*

Badlands Series

Badlands

Lucky Town, A Badlands Novella - *Coming Soon*

The Rising - *Coming Soon*

CPSIA information can be obtained
at www.ICGtesting.com
Printed in the USA
LVHW111646270322
714534LV00001B/139

9 781939 704795